DEATHHUNTER

Also by Ian Watson

The Embedding
The Jonah Kit
The Martian Inca
Alien Embassy
The Very Slow Time Machine
Miracle Visitors
The Gardens of Delight
Under Heaven's Bridge
(with Michael Bishop)
Converts

DEATHHUNTER

A SCIENCE FICTION NOVEL

IAN WATSON

St. Martin's Press
New York

AUTHOR'S NOTE

Part of this novel appeared, in different
form, in *Omni* magazine as a story
entitled "A Cage for Death."

Library of Congress Cataloging in Publication Data

Watson, Ian, 1943-
  Deathhunter.

  I. Title.   II. Title: Death hunter.
PR6073.A863D4 1986   823'.914   86-13024
ISBN 0-312-18556-1

First published in Great Britain by Victor Gollancz Ltd.

First U.S. Edition

10 9 8 7 6 5 4 3 2 1

For Michael Bishop,
fellow bridger of Heaven and the Atlantic

DEATHHUNTER

ONE

As THE SINGLE-CAR monorail train from Gracchus sped out of the last black tunnel into the honeyed sunlight of the valley, Jim Todhunter caught his first sight of Egremont, and his heart rejoiced.

The valley and its community looked as idyllic as their reputation, and if Jim regretted the suddenness of his reassignment from Gracchus, with the consequent interruption of his death researches in the city, to be sent to Egremont could hardly be regarded as a punishment. On the contrary, it seemed more like a consolation prize.

Jim unfolded the local map which Noel Resnick, Master of the House of Death in Egremont, had sent him just before his departure. While the monorail car sighed down towards the suburbs he tried to match the configurations of the map to the rich detail of the scene before him.

Except where a few green tongues of pine and fir forest encroached, the surrounding hills were a glory of orange, red and gold. To the north glinted the blue mirror of Lake Tulane over the dam. Even at this distance he thought he could make out the red and yellow butterflies of racing yachts.

An inviting scene indeed: orchards, farms, tree-lined avenues ruddy with the fall of the year, fountains splashing spouts of silver outside apartment blocks, little electric vehicles beetling about, the public transport pods swinging along a wire like beads, the geodesic domes of the micro-electronics factories . . .

And Downtown itself: which building was which? Was that the cable TV station or the Census Office? Which was the House of Death? Realizing that he was wasting this virgin moment, he tucked the map away as the train began to slow down automatically.

Jim was the only passenger. He wore a red bow-tie, loosely knotted: a dandyish touch which offset his otherwise plain suit — dun-coloured, appropriate to a death guide. However, the mood of his costume was not dour; it was quite unlike the gloom of priestly black. It suggested, perhaps, sand dunes coming into being and passing away in the wind, always changing, giving way to others. Jim's sand dune, though, was speckled with fire at the throat.

He stretched his legs from the two-hour journey, then stood — bowing slightly — and hauled down his valise. He was a tall, raven-haired man in his late thirties, with a permanent slight stoop as though he never trusted doorways to be quite high enough to let him through.

A woman waited on the platform. This must be Marta Bettijohn, whom Resnick had promised would meet him. She was a cheerful, plumpish person with a rosy face and bright blue eyes. A buxom woman. She wore a yellow corduroy dress and brown tweed jacket. In her buttonhole was the silver insignia of the House of Death.

Jim tapped his own little silver rosette with his thumb, and grinned. He dropped the valise, and the two of them shook hands.

"A wonderful day, Jim! And a specially wonderful day for Egremont."

He was taken aback.

"That sounds excessively flattering."

"Oh, I didn't mean . . .! Oh, I'm sorry — of course we're all delighted to have you here! But Jim, what I meant was: Norman Harper is retiring today. Our P and J: our Pride and Joy! Didn't you know that? The TV people will be beaming *this* ceremony out everywhere." She glanced at her watch. "I couldn't possibly miss it."

"Well, I'll be —! I must have missed the announcement. I've been pretty busy these last few days."

She nodded. "I understand."

"Well, well! Quite an auspicious moment to arrive, indeed! Norman Harper, eh? Of course, I knew that he lived here in Egremont . . . Who's in charge of his death, in the House?" As soon as he had said this, Jim regretted it. It sounded as though he imagined that he ought to walk in and guide the poet's death by rights just because he had come from the city. The remark smacked of pretension or vanity, but Marta Bettijohn seemed not to notice.

8

"How can any of us really guide *his* death?" she said. "Alice Huron is the lucky one, but I guess she'll learn more from him than he from her. Not that Alice isn't *good* — I don't mean that. But he's, well, Norman Harper. He'll show *her* the way."

Then Marta proceeded to show Jim the way: out of the station to a waiting electric runabout. Jim folded himself awkwardly into the passenger seat. Overhead, Egremont people were waiting briefly on the Beadway platform and hopping into transport pods that came by at half-minute intervals.

"This is Harper Street," announced Marta proudly, as the runabout purred forward over a pastel mosaic of rubbery tiles. She pointed out the Farming Co-op and the Library, both in neo-classical style, the latter conveniently near the school complex: a glass and steel design resembling several ziggurats colliding with each other. Of course, most of the Library's stock could be accessed directly on screen, she explained; but the borrowing of actual books was encouraged in Egremont — another example of Norman Harper's influence over the community. A poem couldn't be entirely appreciated on a screen.

As they passed the complex, a class of children was spilling out, laughing and shouting. Or perhaps a mixture of several classes, for there were older faces and younger faces. The children waved to the runabout, and Marta waved back as the youngsters raced up the steps of another Beadway terminal.

"I'm a guide at the school," Marta told Jim. "Most of the kids will be watching Norman's retirement on screen, but we'll have some of them there in person: youth bidding adieu to age. Not too many, though! This isn't a circus."

"Hardly!"

"We held a class lottery. It's something they'll always remember. Down there is the Mall — you've heard of our Mall?"

It was a long cross-avenue, arcaded in crystal. Ferns, trees and tall cacti grew in troughs between the shops for as far as Jim could see, and at intervals milky fountains sprayed. Only a few people were about in the Mall this afternoon.

"You really must try the Three Spires restaurant down there. Finest food around: fish, French and country style."

"You'll be my guest?"

Marta wagged a finger at him.

"Oh, I wasn't hinting. Besides — I oughtn't to tell you yet, or you'll hardly keep your mind on Norman's ceremony — but we've fixed up a 'get-to-know-you' barbecue out at the lake this evening. Grilled trout! And a few bottles of the local white, from the Vinehouse."

"Sounds great."

They passed the Peace Office, an octagonal edifice in stone with a massive portico and a gravelled courtyard where standard bay trees alternated with cypresses in large terracotta pots. A few marble statues stood about like pillars of salt. Or like the frozen dead, erect. But there wouldn't be any freezer freaks in Egremont. This community was happily adjusted . . . Perhaps that was why he had been transferred here: so that some of the adjustment could rub off?

"I'll have to check in there."

"No hurry, Jim — not this afternoon! You'll see quite a few of the officers at the ceremony, anyway. A thousand guests — that needs handling with dignity and honour."

A further five minutes' drive brought them to the House of Death itself. Here passengers were descending from the Beadway every half-minute, down on to the wide gravel paths between the green lawns. Thirty or forty runabouts were already parked on the concourse between the House and the Hospital.

Both the Hospital and the House were stone and glass pyramids with gardens growing up over them, tier above tier. The coiled serpent of the physician rose from the peak of the first, and from the tip of the second its partner, the familiar and friendly insignia: a silver rosette, with all the petals of life gathered at just the right moment.

A blue moat flowed around the House of Death, dappled with water-lily leaves bearing one or two late blooms. A single bridge crossed this water of detachment. From a grassy knoll in a far corner of the grounds a thin line of smoke rose like incense, beneath which would be the crematorium, Jim decided. A faint odour of synthetic sandalwood hung in the air. A small domed pavilion of contemplation, in marble, stood in another corner; a few elderly people and a pale child were watching the gathering crowd from it.

A dais had been erected on the main lawn with half a dozen

chairs and a microphone. Music was issuing from remote loud-speakers: a golden Brandenburg Concerto. As the thousand spectators were marshalled by Peace Officers in their white uniforms into receding rows, cross-legged, upon the turf, six people filed up to the dais and sat listening to the music of Bach.

"Come along."

Marta tugged Jim by the arm, down through the ranks of the audience to the very front. They settled themselves on the short soft grass.

"That's Norman Harper on the left," whispered Marta.

"I recognize the face."

"Of course."

Norman Harper was a stocky, white-haired man with rutted features like eroded limestone. His eyes twinkled infectiously.

"And Noel. Noel Resnick."

The Master of the House was a big, burly man, but even so there was a considered, conscious grace about his movements and gestures that seemed to render his weight negligible. Jim thought that there was something vaguely cartoon-like about Noel Resnick — as though an elephant should take up ballet dancing and so completely mesmerize its audience that it fully convinced them of its gracefulness. Resnick looked pleased with himself.

"That's Alice Huron on the right."

Jim stared at the woman who was to guide the poet. She had long black glossy hair, dark eyes, an equine nose, and a pronounced chin. Her fingers were noticeably long and slender, with several chunky rings on them. She must be almost six feet tall, which saved her chin from seeming too exaggerated, as did the fact that she held herself perfectly upright — without any of Jim's defensive stoop. He found himself envying her: both for her coming duty, and for her deportment. Door lintels would raise their hats to her, instead of trying to bump her brow.

"And Lama Ananda." A shaven-headed, saffron-robed man. Possibly he was just a westerner in eastern dress.

"Dr Claudio Menotti — our chief euthanaser." The fat, ruddy-faced fellow exuded bonhomie; he looked like an operatic baritone.

"And Mayor Barnes. Mark Barnes."

The Mayor of Egremont was a tall, middle-aged negro with a

11

neatly-shaped vandyke beard. He appeared to scan the few fleecy clouds in the sky, wondering whether they could possibly have the impertinence to cast a few spots of rain down on the occasion. It hardly looked likely, though. Then the Mayor glanced round as though checking the whereabouts of the news gatherers, who stood with electronic cameras locked on their shoulders and aiming lenses pasted to their foreheads.

The music continued until everyone, including the children, had arrived and settled.

Finally Mayor Barnes rose, and silence fell.

"Friends," he began. His voice was proud and passionate.

TWO

"THE MISSILES ARE all gone, the doomsday machines are dismantled, the day of the gun is over — long since! But we'll never forget the debt that we owe to people like Norman Harper, who helped to make this possible . . ."

The poet inclined his head modestly. Perhaps he only saw himself as a poet, but to other people he was a legislator of mankind — an acknowledged one.

"We were going to destroy the whole of this fair world of ours and all the people in it because we couldn't come to terms with death. Death was something that never happened to us, but only to the other fellow. We expelled the dead from our lives. We made them into strangers, who had nothing to do with us. We pushed death abroad beyond our personal frontier — into enemy territory. And when that happened, strangers — foreigners — all spelt death to us. Oh, we fantasized about an afterlife, even about reincarnation, but we never gave a thought to the business of our own dying which brings this life to an end . . ."

Jim sat up and took notice. The Mayor's speech was going out across the whole land. In view of the recent accident in Gracchus, did this represent the opening word in a campaign against afterlife studies? To be sure, the idea that a soul might survive enriched the death encounter of those people who still believed in such a thing. So the notion of survival had its discreet uses. But if people could hope to survive death, wasn't that equivalent to a denial of death?

12

"*Defence* — which was actually all directed against Death the Stranger — became one of the biggest forces on Earth. And oh boy, did we prosper! Did we get rich, on the bombs and warplanes and bullets! And what a lot of media fun we got from the spectacle of the other fellow's death!"

If there was a campaign in embryo, perhaps it was directed against the freezer freaks? No frozen body had ever been revived, or ever would be, and the few rich people who opted for this course invariably retired from life gracefully. Still, they represented a kind of privileged opposition to the Houses of Death and the policy of timely euthanasia. Possibly some of these people imagined that they could 'live through' the age of Good Death into some future death-denying era? That might well be their secret ambition. But obviously they did not believe in the survival of a soul, or else they would not have had themselves frozen when they became fatally ill or when the Census Office pulled their card. The soul was a horse of a different colour.

A horse — or a nightmare?

"Friends, we thrived on war — because the survivors of a war had magically defeated death. Soldier boys returning home were our immortals. They'd put off the evil hour. They'd outlived the other side. So we began to plan the biggest war of all — the total war. If we could live through the doomsday of the whole darn world, we really would have punched death in the eye! And we would just have been punching *ourselves* in the eye, hitting out at the death that is in all of us . . ."

"Too true," murmured Marta Bettijohn, and Jim nodded automatically. He wished he could totally believe. The afternoon was so golden. The fact that Norman Harper had chosen to retire on the very day that Jim arrived in Egremont was surely a sign.

But had the poet exactly *chosen* to retire? Or had he been encouraged, as a political example . . .? Jim rejected the thought. Norman Harper looked absolutely at peace with himself. Maybe the 'campaign' was all in Jim's imagination. Everything that Mayor Barnes said was so true. One day, when death really was second nature to everyone, perhaps this sort of oratory could wither away because it had become unnecessary.

Looking round at the audience, Jim realized the extent to which

13

death had already become second nature, particularly for the younger people present. He felt momentarily like an anachronism, something out of date; then he shucked off the sensation. The sun shone down, gilding his spirit. He too was a guide in the House of Death, and a good one. He concentrated on believing — in the path which had saved perhaps a third of the human race from the fate of the rest. How could he be an anachronism? The world had been this way for most of his life.

"But some people understood: people like our own Norman Harper. They got us to shake hands with friendly, natural death again. Along with some others — who equally deserve our praise and thanks — he started the great movement which has led to the Houses of Death and the reconstruction of our whole society. So at last the Big Fear went away. Now that we accept the death that is part of us, we have a future again. For that we thank you, Norman, from the heart."

Mayor Barnes sat down, to quiet applause.

"The man's eloquent," whispered Marta. "He could be a guide himself."

"No, he's an orator, a politician. You shouldn't make speeches to the dying."

"Well, of course not. But even so."

Noel Resnick, Master of the House, rose next. He performed a slow mesmeric dance about the focal point of the microphone while he spoke, lifting himself up on right tiptoes then on left tiptoes. Jim recalled that stutterers occasionally 'danced' like this to lose their stutter.

". . . there was no dialogue with one's own death," Resnick was saying in a firm voice. "Consequently so-called 'men of good will' spoke out against this country, or that group of people. Traitors were sought and pilloried as scapegoats. All this, because these men of 'good will' placed their own death *out there*. They drove it like a stake into the hearts of the enemies they manufactured. Confrontation and victory were the watchwords. So was 'putting up a fight' — for freedom, for the individual, you name it — even if it meant mass death for everybody. And the real name of their enemy was always Death itself. But it just so happens that there is no enemy alien named 'Death'. There is no war. There is no other side. There is only here, and us."

14

Obviously Resnick too was something of a politician. Was he in competition with Mayor Barnes? The answer hardly interested Jim, yet he noted the existence of a question. He noted, too, that this Resnick was a tough Master — even if he had overcome a stutter, and perhaps because of this. The Master of the larger House of Death in Gracchus had been more sympathetic and flexible; but even he had put his foot down in the end.

A flight of wild ducks winged overhead in a V formation. How did the ducks learn to fly with such perfect symmetry? Why, in much the same way that a young child learns the symmetry of day and night, and of waking and sleeping. In its infant brain the child decides that there must exist a corresponding cycle of life and death too. As death follows life, so must another life follow death . . .

Was this really such a false decision, if the same instinctive sense of symmetry guided the wild ducks in their flight?

Jim shook his head as though to clear it of delusions — to shake the malaise of the old deluded days which he had hardly even known.

Instead, he concentrated on the jolly solidity of Marta Bettijohn — and on being in this crowd which could genuinely celebrate death as part of life. And especially he concentrated on the focus of their celebrations, the white-haired poet whom they all honoured on this, his last day in the public world.

Presently, Resnick ceased to sway about before the microphone like a vast pendulum bob, and sat down. Norman Harper stood, and embraced his audience with outstretched, gnarled hands.

"It's my day to retire," he said affectionately. "I shall not make a speech." He chuckled softly. "How could I compete with what has gone before? Instead, let me simply quote a favourite passage from my own *Book of Death*."

The poet closed his eyes. Like blind Homer he recited.

"The embryo bird must partly die
If its wings are to emerge, to fly.
The caterpillar dies, as well,
To become the butterfly, so swell.
While man himself dies every seven
Years, but goes not up to heaven.

So here is death, and here is life:
These Siamese twins shall know no strife . . ."

"Doggerel," muttered Jim, despite himself.
"Hush!" said Marta. "What did you say?"
"Nothing, sorry."

"Each life is several generations
Of births and deaths like transit stations;
And then the train returns at last
To where it started, in the past.
Our death is in us, not 'out there';
It grows out of us, like our hair.
It falls like hair, like Autumn leaves;
And in the earth new life achieves.
There is no Enemy, no Thief:
A dangerous and a false belief!
Many times in life we die
So that our new mind-wings can fly;
And when we finally fold those wings,
Our spirit sings, then dies away.
There is no more; there is no Sting.
We shall be as we were before.
The day is over, perfect day . . ."

Someone — a man — pushed roughly between Jim and Marta. The man ran to the front of the dais, where Norman Harper continued to recite, unaware of the disturbance.

The intruder raised his right hand. Something resembling a pipe stem was clutched in it.

A sharp crack sounded, then a second crack — no louder than two branches snapping underfoot.

Blood bloomed on Norman Harper's throat and chest. Gagging, the poet staggered backwards. He crashed into the chair which he had been occupying so calmly just a few minutes earlier. Chair and poet plunged off the back of the dais on to the lawn. Both lay motionless.

Uncomprehending silence followed, for a few moments. During this pause the intruder lowered his right hand. He let what he held

16

fall to the turf. Then somebody screamed, and someone else.

Marta seized Jim's arm. Her fingers squeezed him cruelly.

"He — *murdered* — Norman!" she cried in Jim's face. "He
. . . a *handgun*!"

There was a huge incongruity about what had happened. It was
like a TV play — but no TV play like this had been made or
screened for many years. It was something from the proscribed
archives. Jim sat dumbly watching it. The lead actor — the murderer — seemed to have little idea what to do now that he had
performed his act. Nobody else seemed to have much idea what to
do about him.

Back in the audience people were scrambling and shouting and
crashing into each other. Mayor Barnes jumped up, knocking his
own chair over. Leaping down from the dais, he knelt beside the
poet, looking appalled. Dr Menotti joined him. Resnick rose too,
and began oscillating back and forth on the platform in indecision.
Alice Huron started to weep. The woman dragged her hair over her
face like some ancient mourner. In full view of everyone she wept
privately, as though her tears could wash away what had just
happened. But no one was noticing her except for Jim. Somehow,
she noticed Jim's eyes upon her. Abruptly she calmed, seeming to
freeze her feelings, and directed a quick look of hatred at him for
what he had seen.

Breaking Marta's grip as gently as he could, Jim scrambled to his
feet. He took a few steps towards the murderer. But what should he
do? Strike him to the ground? Pinion him? The murderer stood
passively. While the murderer waited and Jim hesitated, two Peace
Officers arrived and an attendant from the House ran over. These
three men positioned themselves around the killer like chess pieces
checking yet unable to capture the king. Jim bent and retrieved the
gun. Its touch felt utterly strange, as though it had fallen from the
stars. He handed it to one of the officers, who quickly hid it in his
pocket.

A news gatherer was moving in now, filming the face of the killer
— which was like a starving animal's, thin and worn. It wore an
expression of impassive despair — of a prey cornered by a
predator. Yet the eyes were still looking for some exit. They hunted
for some crack to slip through — but not for a crack in the real
world, since no such crack existed. They looked for a crack in the

17

order of things itself, as though the act of killing had been a magical gesture, a conjuration which might call up some rescuing demon out of a sudden hole in the ground. The murderer was in his fifties, and nearly bald: he was a field gone sterile. What little hair he had was grey. He wore one of the yellow tunics of a resident in the House of Death.

As the TV man moved right up to him, he addressed the camera:

> "There goes he,
> Instead of me,"

said the killer wryly.

"You see, I can make up poems too."

"Stop filming!" Resnick shouted from the dais. "Stop recording!"

The news gatherer obediently switched off his camera. However, his colleague round on the other side of the dais had not heard and continued to film the sprawled body of the poet. The newsman was like a simple robot which could not tell when the task set it had become grossly inappropriate. Noticing, and cursing, Resnick dealt with him too.

Presently, touching the killer as little as possible — as though he was red-hot or radioactive — the two officers and the attendant shepherded him away in the direction of the House.

Jim rejoined Marta. She was on her hands and knees. Someone must have knocked her over and now — too shocked to stand up on her own — she needed the support of all four limbs. She seemed to be hunting for something lost in the grass — her beliefs?

Offering her his hand, Jim hauled her up and supported her.

"I guess," gasped Marta, "we won't get out to the lake this evening." She concentrated on this disappointment, rather than on the grotesque scene which the celebration had become. This clearly restored a certain sense of reality to her, since what had happened had been quite unreal.

She smiled coaxingly.

"I'd better show you your rooms in the House." She squeezed Jim's hand.

"Well, I'll be —!" thought Jim. Did she want him to make love to her, to burn out the awful experience? He knew that death was a kind of lover to some women. But what had happened here this afternoon had been an act of rape . . .

18

THREE

AFTER COLLECTING HIS valise from the runabout, Jim walked back with Marta to the stone bridge over the moat. Twin sculptures flanked the way across: aluminium-winged butterflies a couple of feet high, mounted on white marble hourglasses. Gusts of wind set these butterflies rotating like the turnstiles of an auto-shop.

Following the ceremony of honour, the poet ought to have crossed this same bridge to separate himself from life in Egremont, and presently — in days or weeks, at the discretion of Alice Huron and his own inner promptings — from life itself. Right now the two metal butterflies looked like great sharp spinning knives to Jim. The murder had contaminated everything precious.

The glass doors whispered apart, and they entered a crowded foyer. At least a score of residents had gathered here. Voices were raised, some shrill and fearful, others angry and complaining. The whole death sequence of these clients had been set back. But at least they had taken refuge in the House, and an attendant and a guide were doing their best to soothe the situation.

Marta hurried Jim through the small crowd and led him along to the elevator core. They rose up to the twelfth tier.

This high up the pyramid there was space for just four staff apartments, one at each point of the compass. Jim's new home faced west. As Marta held the door open for him, the westering sun was flooding through the canted glass louvres, dappling the local pine furnishings with shadows of yucca, holly, firethorn and fuchsia that grew outside on the balcony. Perspex privacy baffles stood at the north- and south-west corners of this balcony, and through the aerial garden was a view of distant suburbs fading into farmland.

The lounge opened on to a bedroom with white venetian blinds. Jim dumped his bag on the bed. Returning to the lounge, he switched on the TV set.

Mayor Barnes stood addressing the camera. To judge by a backdrop of slanted glass and rose bushes with white blooms, he was being filmed elsewhere in the House.

Barnes? Had Resnick made a fool of himself by shouting at the news gatherers? True, the electronic news would have been subject to a thirty second delay loop for better editing before transmission — though the first vivid, blood-stained images of the poet crashing back on to the turf would have gone out as filmed; everyone had been struck dumb, to begin with.

Barnes looked quietly composed.

". . . but we must not simply grieve at the manner in which Norman Harper has been cheated of his own good death. I believe that Norman would have wished us all to *rededicate* ourselves to the ideals represented by these Houses — especially if we hail from the unreconstructed era when a person's death had no place in the social system but was something outside of it, something alien. If we suspect that we are polluted by the false programming of the old days — if we feel a mad ambition in ourselves to be frozen, or reincarnated, or translated on to some astral plane to avoid the truth of our life's end — why don't we all visit our local House of Death to discover the beauty of dying at the proper time? Why don't we sign on for a seminar? The Houses are places of detachment, yes indeed — but they are not outside of the community. In a real sense they are its heart. The dying are often happy to share their experiences . . ."

'More work,' thought Jim wryly: more open-house seminars for the public, in addition to the school and TV presentations. Conducted discreetly, of course. Sensitively. Without infringing the right to privacy of any of the clients. But still, more work . . .

Mentally, he rapped himself over the knuckles for pride and selfishness.

"The alternative is to harbour *murder* in one's bosom — and we've seen what comes of that today. The person who denies death is someone who mentally destroys the world for others. As Norman Harper wrote elsewhere in his *Book of Death*, 'You should go gently into that good night . . .' "

"I told you he could be a guide," said Marta.

"He's using the event."

20

"On the contrary, he's *defusing* it. He's preventing a domino effect. Don't you realize how dangerous this is? It's the first violence there's been on any screen for years! How many kids have had their feelings scrambled by what they saw today? And how about all the poor, disturbed people who have trouble adjusting in any case? It was a direct attack on . . . everything."

"Do you think it was planned as such?"

"Of course not."

"In that case, you're exaggerating. A few people still do murder other people. It happens in the cities, you know. The murder rate is very, very low, and falling. But it isn't zero."

"And it *never* should be news. Not one single killing should be news."

Jim shrugged. "This one is."

Marta moved closer to him, and touched his arm.

He said gently, "I can't banish this from you, you know? I'd be taking the place of Death, if I tried. But Death *isn't* anyone — neither seducer, nor executioner."

She drew back suddenly.

"That may be your interpretation of my feelings. I find it rather insulting."

"Even so, it's what you feel."

She looked down at the yellow and brown carpet-tiles.

"You're a clever guide," she said. "Perceptive. I guess you must have helped one or two women clients in your time — by proving that the Seducer is only human? Anyhow," she rushed on, not wanting to hear the answer, "what did you mean by muttering 'doggerel' in the middle of Norman's poem?"

"Nothing, really."

"No, tell me."

Jim realized that Marta had achieved a hold over him — an option on his private feelings — which was unfortunate on such brief acquaintance, though it was partly his own fault. It was as though the gunshots had briefly stripped them both naked to each other; and now they remembered each other's nakedness.

"It's just that so many valuable things *did* spring from our death anxieties in the past. So much philosophy. So much art."

"Therefore Norman's poetry isn't really art, because he wasn't anxious? What an ambivalent character you are!"

"Do you mean 'two-faced'? You have to identify with the people you guide, before they can identify with you. Even when they're angry or hostile to start with. Even when they're just protesting . . . at the general lack of protest."

"Why did they *really* transfer you here from Gracchus?"

Jim was saved from answering her by the warble of the telephone. As Jim switched off the TV set, Mayor Barnes disappeared into a point of light which vanished, just as Mayor Barnes and everyone else would when they died . . .

Jim put the phone down.

"That was Resnick."

"So I gathered."

"I'm to see him in half an hour. Apparently he wants me to guide the killer — because I'm uninvolved. I'm not of Egremont. So I won't feel any personal bitterness. I guess that answers your question, Marta. They transferred me here from Gracchus so that I could guide Norman Harper's murderer."

He consulted his watch. If Marta still nursed the desires that he suspected, they were not to be fulfilled this afternoon . . .

"How very ironic you can be," she said.

The greater irony, he thought, was that his own brief earlier fantasy of guiding Norman Harper had come true so suddenly, yet at one hideous remove.

Jim walked to the door as though to open it for Marta. Once there, he merely stood and patted its frame. He felt possessed by an imp of the perverse.

"I wonder if Death's doorway will let me pass when my time comes?" he asked her, darkly. "Or might I get stuck in it? Half-way in and half-way out? Perhaps the old legends of Zombies are really based on people who get stuck in that doorway. Their conscious mind has gone through, but the automatic mind is left on our side, still running the body — how about that?"

Surprisingly, she joined in his humour.

"So the freezer freaks are zombies on ice — now there's an idea!"

"I sometimes wonder if we guides are not the new immortals? Deep down in our minds, I mean. We see everyone else on their way. But we stay here: the privileged door-keepers."

22

She shook her head firmly. "We have our time and season too. Without *that*, we'd be . . . well, we'd be . . ."

"We'd be executioners, if we didn't retire when that sixtieth year comes round."

"And even sooner sometimes . . ."

"Oh yes, if a guide gets saturated with the seductive beauty of dying."

"I don't quite understand you, Jim — but I hope we're going to be good colleagues, and friends."

Jim chuckled. "To every guide, his own personal touch. Or hers. Mine may be humour, for those who need humour. It may even be farce! It's an approach that can work wonders with some people. There are some clients who hate to be contemplative about their demise."

"They can be *shown*."

"They still think it's sanctimonious. And other people are actually scared. For them, a joke can be a fine nerve tonic. What did William Blake say? 'Mirth braces; bliss relaxes'? Well, if he didn't, he ought to have. He died laughing, didn't he? Or was it singing? Norman Harper never quite . . ."

"Quite what?"

"Quite wrote poetry like Blake."

"Norman wrote for an audience of real people, not for his own fevered, mystical brain." Marta placed her hands on her hips defiantly. "I wish you joy of cracking jokes with his killer!" Yet she stood thus only for a moment. To Jim it was clear that she couldn't tolerate harsh words — least of all her own.

"You're a strange person," she said quietly, almost caressingly. "Maybe it takes a strange person to guide someone who did . . . what that creature did today."

"It's nice to know I have my uses."

"We all *do*. Everyone's death has its own precious usefulness."

"As Mayor Barnes said just now, of Norman Harper's."

Jim touched Marta lightly on the shoulder. As he well knew from experience with the dying and with those on the path to voluntary death, one moment of such contact spoke volumes of persuasion.

"Will you show me the refectory? I'd like a cup of coffee before I meet Resnick."

Outside the window, the yucca leaves were green knives. Their shadows stabbed the furniture. The fuchsia flowers were drops of blood.

FOUR

RESNICK DRAPED AN arm over Jim's stooped shoulders, giving the impression of a circus impresario comforting a would-be hunchback who had the misfortune to be taller than most other people. Thus he drew Jim across the room towards a large bean-bag style seat. A seat like a pitcher plant; once in, it would be difficult to struggle out again. Jim subsided into it.

Since the Master's office, lit by fluorescents, was deep inside the body of the House one entire wall was devoted to a scene-screen. A sunset seascape opened illusorily out of the office. A woolpack sky was afire with red and salmon-pink; an orange sun balanced exactly on the sea horizon, and a golden road stretched across the waters towards the desk. 'The ocean from whose bourne no traveller returns,' thought Jim.

Alice Huron stood staring along that road. Presently she turned, to acknowledge Jim with a nod, then with a second more thoughtful nod — as she remembered him from the ceremony, he saw.

"You don't mind if Alice stays, do you?" asked Resnick. "She's been . . ."

"Robbed?" prompted Jim.

The Master smiled appreciatively.

"Quite so. The whole House was robbed. Egremont was robbed. In a deeper sense, of course, Norman Harper was most grievously robbed."

" 'There is no Enemy, no Thief,' " quoted Alice bitterly. "But there *was*. Today there was. Norman's death *was* out there. What a horrid, obscene thing." The tall woman summoned a faint smile. "We ought to be welcoming you, Jim. We were planning . . ."

"To have a trout roast — I heard. Don't worry about it."

"We'll still hold one — on Friday. That, I promise you."

And what else was she promising? Her tone implied that she had a minor score to settle with him — for watching her in her moment of weakness, when no one else had eyes for it. But perhaps he was imagining this.

She rounded on Resnick.

"How can that beast possibly go to a good death after this?"

And Jim realized: he himself was now the custodian of the beast, therefore he was a little monstrous in her eyes . . .

"Does one punish a dying man?" parried Resnick. "Does one withhold counselling? Maybe that's what he was hoping for!"

"I presume that 'the beast' has a name," said Jim.

"Weinberger. Nathan Weinberger. He was once a guide himself. He left the House years ago. He rejected his oath and tore up his contract. It was easier to get away with behaviour like that back then. He's been working in micro-electronics since — in Egremont, of course. Until the crab got him."

Cancer.

"How long has he left?"

"Three to four months, maybe less. Obviously he won't have to run *that* course to the very end! We were hoping to guide him out in another week or two. What on earth did he think he was doing? He's set the whole schedule back. It's all so utterly absurd."

"Maybe it isn't absurd to him," said Jim. "As to what he thought he was doing, that's for me to find out, isn't it?"

"Certainly. Absolutely. But this is a major case. All the Houses will be interested. The public too, unfortunately."

"Meaning, am I up to it?"

"Let's see." Resnick keyed the data console on his desk.

"If you hadn't arrived at this timely — or untimely — moment," he said, as he scanned the recessed screen, "we'd have been obliged to call a guide in from outside. *That* would not have looked good. As it is, the whole affair stays securely in this House. Your arrival is . . . yes, timely. I see that you've been involved in some afterlife studies in Gracchus?"

Jim realized with a shock that Resnick was reviewing the Todhunter dossier, not that of . . . what was his name, Weinberger? Reviewing it with a third party, Alice, standing by. Admittedly the Huron woman wasn't looking over Resnick's shoulder — but even so.

"That came to an abrupt end."

"Well, that's the affair of the Gracchus House. Were you hoping to carry on here? My predecessor was interested in such things. He sound-proofed a room down in the basement for astral

— no, I *shan't* use that word!— for monkeying around with trance states: out-of-the-body illusion stuff. You people at Gracchus seem to have been moving in the same direction. As a tactic, I presume, to bolster up weak minds . . .?" Resnick stared hard at Jim. "So what sent you down the afterlife path? What was your own earliest death encounter?"

In common with all guide applicants Jim originally had undertaken self-analysis, aided by hypnosis, of his own childhood discovery of death. The results of this analysis — and consequently the answer to the Master's question — were certainly in the dossier. And the dossier had been transferred from Gracchus to the Egremont computer at least a week ago. Had Resnick not bothered to scan it till now? If not, surely he wouldn't have appointed Jim as guide to Norman Harper's murderer? Unless, of course, he was at his wit's end . . .

He must want to hear the answer from Jim's own lips. One's interpretation of such things sometimes altered as the years went by.

Or was Resnick doing this for Alice Huron's benefit — as a sop to recompense her for her loss of Norman Harper? Or even because . . . she was the real decision-maker hereabouts? Had he left it to someone else to scan the dossier for him: someone who already knew exactly what it said, and who was in the room right now?

Alice Huron was once more inspecting the everlasting sunset, as though Resnick's questions were of no consequence to her. The engorged sun prepared to dip beneath the waters, bringing the darkness of night; but it never actually did so. Jim thought briefly of the freezer freaks, suspended — yet in reality dead. There was nothing of poised golden evening about *their* experience: their complete lack of experience.

Alice Huron. Jim had agreed that she could stay, and now she would eavesdrop on his earliest death encounter — if she was not already privy to it. 'Always check the small print,' he reflected wryly. Already he had got himself into something of a knot with Marta Bettijohn. Why had he allowed a similar situation to develop with this other woman? Because he *wanted* her to be present — having seen her naked, too, when she wept.

At this point Jim decided that Alice must certainly be Resnick's mistress; and he felt an irrational sense of loss at this discovery

— as though somehow she ought to belong to him because they both had to contend with ungenerous doorways.

'I'm eroticising things childishly . . . And imagining the same about other people . . .' Actually, Marta had been doing just that. Quite definitely she had been eroticising this afternoon's tragedy. In many respects a House of Death was an erotic hothouse. Inevitably relationships developed between the guides.

"Well?" asked Resnick.

"I fell into a river," Jim said. "I drowned. I saw the radiance, I experienced bliss. Then they pulled me out and revived me." It had all been a very long time ago, but how clearly the experience remained with him! "I wanted to show other people the same light, and let them know how we can die filled with joy. I wanted to show them how not to be afraid."

And perhaps, through his clients, he had wanted to catch reflected glimpses of that radiance, to be sure that it was still available.

"Mr Ananda considers that the 'death light' is simply a brain reaction: a perception thing," remarked Resnick. "Not a tunnel into heaven. Just something natural, not supernatural."

"It's very valuable to know that you will feel joy at the end."

"Surely. And death therapy has to be tailored to suit the clients, not dogmatised. But really, afterlife research has led nowhere. We mustn't promise falsehoods."

"Doses of opium," muttered Alice.

"Afterlife research has got nowhere for one simple reason," said Jim. "Because no one is brought back from death nowadays. Instead, everyone is eased into it. So there's no evidence. Except for odd cases like mine — rescues from drowning."

"So it's all hypothetical," said Alice sharply. "Fantasies about death are dangerous. They lead to events such as today's."

"Well, I don't dogmatise — I tailor, as Noel so neatly puts it. Though frankly, there *is* a way of glimpsing that light: by death mimicry, by playing possum. That's what was going on in Gracchus: Project Possum."

"Yes, and I hear that one guide played possum so successfully that he did genuinely die," said Resnick. "That's where the real danger in the afterlife concept lies. It can lead to a denial of *this* good world — to a fevered intoxication with some 'other side',

27

and even to suicide, which is violence against society. We've seen enough violence today to last us a lifetime.''

"Where did Weinberger get the gun?" asked Jim, to change the subject.

Resnick dangled a key. "Ask him. He's in room 302."

"Aren't the P.Os questioning him?"

"He retired, remember? He's in *our* custody. I don't think it matters very much where he got the gun. Not all firearms can have been recalled and destroyed. People hang on to the stupidest of things. Medical poisons. Pills. No, it's what he *did* with it. And he did it on his own. Weinberger was a loner, and I guess he was a looney too. But he kept a low profile — right until he popped up on the firing range."

"You've got that the wrong way round," said Alice. "Traditionally, it's the target that pops up."

"Oh well yes, I know that. But who needs a tradition like that?" Resnick swung back to Jim.

"I realize that it's your very first day here . . ."

"I'll get on the job. That's why I came."

"But take your time. Weinberger has to adjust. And *that* can only come from inside him. Obviously he's a very long way off that right now. But people will want to hear that he adjusted successfully, and it'll have to be the truth. At the moment he's a gross example of stage-two anger. He hid it very well — quite as well as he hid the gun! We thought he was into stage-four depression, just prior to acceptance. I suppose his training as an ex-guide helped him mislead us. Here, I'll give you his cassette — you'll want to play it before you visit him."

Hauling himself out of the floppy chair, Jim accepted the cassette and slipped it into his breast pocket along with the room key. He shook his head.

"No, I think I'll see him raw. I'll let *him* tell me who he is."

Resnick nodded affably.

As Jim was opening the door to leave, Alice called, "Friday evening, right? Barbecue time. Let's hope the weather holds."

In the scene-screen behind her, the weather held forever and forever.

FIVE

NATHAN WEINBERGER LAY on his bed, looking at once wild and passive — as though he had been felled by a tranquilliser dart and could only move his eyes now.

But Jim doubted that the man had been sedated. Why would Resnick have insisted on early meeting, if Weinberger was drugged?

No, that wasn't it. Weinberger looked like a paralysed wild animal because he was caged. He alone in all the House was locked in. And anything potentially lethal had been carefully removed from his cell. Jim noted that a camera eye had been plugged in, up near the ceiling, to allow a duty attendant to monitor the room. A small red light glowed by it.

Room 302 was deep within the body of the House, as was usual with rooms for clients supposed to be in the final stages of withdrawal. So, of course, there was a scene-screen: one wall held a deep vista of rolling forests. Yet the Weinberger animal had no way of running off into those forests to hide himself and die alone, unguided. He was penned.

"Hello," said Jim.

The prisoner made no response.

Jim picked up the phone by the bed.

"Guide Todhunter speaking. I require privacy."

A voice grumbled at him briefly, then the red light near the camera went out.

Jim sat by the bed. 'This is a murderer,' he thought. A rare and dangerous beast — a zoo specimen. But the man did not look very dangerous.

"Well, Mr Weinberger — Nathan, if I may — you've certainly made a lot of waves here! The ripples are really spreading out. I don't suppose you're too bothered about who I am, but my name's

Jim Todhunter. I'm your new guide, fresh in from Gracchus — my first day here, in fact. I don't tell you that to gain sympathy votes; just to underline the fact that my mind's wide open to you. So far, all I know about you is that you were once a guide yourself . . ."

Weinberger did look at him now.

"Death Hunter: that's what your name is, fellow. *Tod* is German for death. Do you really know how to hunt for Death?"

"As a guide, do you mean?"

"You don't understand. How could you?" The man closed his wild eyes, as though to blank Jim out from his attention.

"Try me, Nathan."

"This is a sick society," said Weinberger, almost to himself. "I know why it's this way. But nobody understands death."

"Surely it's the first sane society in history, precisely because it takes full account of death? Death is integrated, not locked out."

"Sure, from childhood onwards. It's like a mockery of ancient Egypt nowadays. Only, we don't build pyramid tombs or put golden dishes in them . . . Though I guess this House is a passable imitation of a pyramid. I wonder if that was in the architect's basement of a mind?"

Jim felt tolerably pleased at the way things were going.

"Who would eat off those golden dishes?" he asked lightly. "Only the archeologists of the future."

"Maybe Death could eat off them."

"But death isn't a person."

"Oh, isn't it?"

"You said 'it'. Is a person neuter?"

"If it's Death, fellow."

"Is that how you see death? As the Great Neuterer, equipped with gelding shears instead of a scythe? Not as the Great Fulfiller?"

"See?" echoed Weinberger. "Nobody sees. Everybody's blind."

"Except for you . . ."

"Oh, I haven't seen what I *could* see! It's as though I've got another sense that I don't know how to use. Another few weeks, and it would have been a different story! But I got retired, by the factory. The medical net caught me. Here I am."

"Why did you kill Norman Harper?"

"Maybe because he was a puffed-up bore. Or because he was the figurehead of lies. Or maybe I did it to save him."

"Save him? Whatever from?"

"From Death, of course. Death gets everybody nowadays — apart from those lucky few who get squashed by a truck when they're looking the wrong way. Or get electrocuted. The fast ones who get taken by surprise. Even drowning's probably a bit too slow."

"I drowned, Nathan. When I was a boy. I really did drown, and they revived me. I experienced . . . bliss."

"Like a shot of heroin? If you remember what heroin was. Death gets everybody nowadays. The signals are all hot and strong. It hears them all, it smells them all."

"If you think that death's like an addictive drug, I might point out that everyone has always died! What difference is there nowadays, except that we know how to approach death in the best frame of mind? And when to."

"Death didn't get everyone, once. Death missed a whole lot of people. They weren't in the right frame of mind. They weren't putting out the right signals. Their minds were still fighting their bodies — still refusing them permission. Now it's too easy for Death — it's plain sailing. Death grows strong. It grows strong, fellow. It runs the whole damn world, or what's left of it. It must have been able to get inside our heads to fix things this way."

Weinberger was certainly talkative enough now, but what he was saying seemed not so much insane as inexplicable. This primitive personalising of death should have been washed out of him long ago, especially since he had trained in a House of Death himself. And left it, Jim reminded himself. And torn up his covenant. Weinberger was obviously in a severe rejection phase — mixed up with a desire to negotiate with 'Death', and even sacrifice to 'him', or 'it'. (Yes, 'it': Death was a non-person for him.) All in all, it was a very odd throwback to the old days.

"You've got it all worked out," said Jim neutrally.

"The best defence against Death," observed Weinberger quite suddenly, "is war and murder and accidents. The very best defence of all would be a hydrogen bomb."

"Oh, I *see*."

"No, you don't. I know perfectly well how you classify that sort

31

of remark. 'Wars and riots indicate our decreasing ability to face death with acceptance and dignity.' Unquote. But maybe there's more than one kind of death.''

"Well, of course there is —"

"Death as per the Houses, and the unregulated, anarchic sort of death? No, it isn't that simple.''

"Tell me then, Nathan.''

Weinberger gazed into the phantom forests opening from his prison. He shook his head.

"I weary, Guide Todhunter. I despair. Go and hunt Death yourself, somewhere else. And just hope that you don't find it, till the big surprise comes along. Then you'll have led a rewarding, well-balanced, if moronic life — just as Norman Harper did. I saved Harper from himself. One owes a duty to fools. Go on, now. And get that spy-eye switched back on.''

"The camera's perfectly understandable, isn't it?'' Jim picked up the phone and spoke briefly. The red light blinked on again. 'Don't argue with the dying,' he thought. 'I've accomplished enough for one visit. Weinberger sends me away now — but only so that we can carry on when I return.'

"I'll be back. Tomorrow morning, if I may?''

"Do you know, I really ought to have shot myself, not him? But that wouldn't have worked out at all — unless I could have taken myself by surprise! That camera's quite unnecessary. You could fill this whole room with knives and ropes and bottles of poison. I wouldn't touch them.''

"I think we'll stick with the camera, hmm? Now, what time should I call back in the morning?''

"Oh, the consolations of choice! Okay, let's play it by the book! Make it ten-thirty.''

Once he had left the room and locked it, Jim realized that he had forgotten to ask Weinberger about the gun. Yet this hardly seemed important, compared with his client's incredibly distorted view of life and death which — somehow — Jim had to get straightened out.

SIX

PROMPTLY AT TEN-THIRTY the next morning Jim knocked on Weinberger's door. He had found nothing on Weinberger's cassette to account for his behaviour, beyond his unexplained defection from the House of Death some ten years earlier. He had checked, too, that his client had already been fed and medicated and had his bed made up, just in case the staff felt inclined to shun the murderer or give him short shrift. However, this had not happened.

Silence greeted his knock. But Jim still waited a moment, considerately, before unlocking the door. He walked in to meet Weinberger's expectant stare. The man said nothing, though.

After phoning for privacy, Jim sat down.

The scene-screen showed the same rolling forests as on the previous day. Jim toyed with the idea of asking Weinberger whether he would care for a change of scene. It would be a weak gambit, he decided. Anyway, the last thing that a dying man should crave was the stimulation of novelty. If Weinberger felt likewise, surely this was one good sign.

Jim opted for a strong gambit, instead.

"I'm *not* going to play this by the book, Nathan."

The book in question being *Good Death: The Guidance of the Dying* — by now in its twelfth revised edition. No doubt Weinberger would have some earlier edition practically by heart.

"I want you to tell me exactly what you meant, yesterday: 'Go and hunt death, and just hope you don't find it.' But I shall tell you my own feelings first. Frankly, I have my own reservations about what's going on in the Houses these days. For instance, I suspect there'll be a crackdown on any kind of afterlife studies for political reasons. It's as though any proof of an afterlife would throw society off course, so that we mustn't even entertain the idea.

33

Myself, I don't think an afterlife is something that can ever be proved. It's a grey area, like the question of where the universe came from, or where it will go after it collapses. But I really believe the afterlife option should be kept open — whilst we still guide people to good deaths as the final end of life.''

"That sounds like one almighty contradiction,'' said Weinberger. Jim noted the interest in his voice.

"Not really. The least likely thing about any afterlife would be continuity of *personal* experience. Why? Because it's the *person* who dies. Just suppose that all the memories of everything you experienced in life survived: in what context would they survive? As a sort of tape-loop repeating itself endlessly with no fresh input? A sort of animated scene-screen of your life? Hardly! On the other hand, if there *is* new experience, how long would it be before you were totally swamped with this fresh input — which had *no connection* with this life of ours? So there may be something after death, but it isn't a continuation of all this. And it isn't a repetition. We have to accept the closure of the here and now.''

"You saw the light of bliss when you drowned. And now that's what you expect, isn't it? A sort of eternal orgasm?''

"I'd rather call it an enlightenment. But I'm glad you mentioned eternity. Our time sense depends upon the metabolic rate of the body, doesn't it? So a child experiences an hour as a much larger span of time than an adult does. Time shrinks as we grow older. The higher up the pyramid of life we are, the narrower it becomes. Now, what if there's a sudden reversal at the moment of death? Or what if we reach a point of no-time, and all-time? What if the instant of death is an *eternal* moment to the person experiencing it? What if it goes on and on forever, for us, even though the ordinary world cremates us and moves on at its usual average pace?''

"So the afterlife would be the last fading second — but it just goes on and on? What a mad idea! Listen, fellow, Death waits for us — but sometimes we get past it. Sometimes we're too fast for it.''

"Too fast?''

"Norman Harper went too quickly — thanks to me. So he got through.''

Jim shook his head in bewilderment.

"Through *what*?''

"Have you ever heard of corpse-sweat, Mr Todhunter? Alias: the pheromone of death?"

"I know what pheromones are," said Jim. "They're chemicals which living creatures secrete to influence other living creatures. For instance, sexual attractor pheromones: those attract males or females — and then they switch off the opposition."

Weinberger sat up. "They're the most powerful substances in nature. A single molecule five miles downwind will bring a moth flying to the female that released it. Let me tell you something, fellow. There's a pheromone of death: a substance which people release when they're close to dying. It attracts Death to them. And Death harvests them. Originally I guess it evolved as a warning signal. It tells other members of the species, 'Something's dying here. Danger! Clear off!' It had survival value. And then carrion eaters learned how to home in on it. How do you suppose that vultures know when to gather? No one ever explained that to my satisfaction. The answer's obvious, if there's a pheromone of death. And there is. That's what corpse-sweat is: the stuff released by the dying body, and the dying mind. Of course, you begin releasing it before you're actually a corpse. But we're damn poor as a species at reading body signals, so nobody has ever really noticed it. Not consciously."

Weinberger's eyes were wild, obsessed.

"The pheromone warns — but it attracts as well. It attracts Death to the dying. Death is the soul-vulture, Jim."

Jim noted the use of his first name, but he was too stunned by Weinberger's fantasy to feel really thankful.

"You're saying that there's a parasite — a creature that feeds on our deaths? A thing that eats souls? And because we prepare everyone for death in the Houses, no one is getting through its net?"

"The victims of sudden accidents get through. The victims of murder. Maybe I ought to be saying the 'beneficiaries' of murder and accident."

"That's a pretty wild assertion."

"Oh, I can prove it. Or rather, I was getting to the point of proving it. Then the crab got me by the claw. Now there isn't time."

"Have you told this to anyone else?"

35

Weinberger laughed dismissively.

"People are too banal. They're too ordinary, to accept that their world's really upside-down and inside-out."

"I'm glad you feel you can confide in me."

"Do you know why I quit the House? To pursue my own research! They would never have let me do it here. It's the same with you. Where have your afterlife studies got to? And you aren't even looking in the right ball court."

"Do you suppose that Death — Mister D — is somehow censoring research into his nature?"

"Not 'his' nature. I'm not that dumb. I don't know the answer to that question — except maybe. All I managed to do in this House was collect enough corpse-sweat, secretly, to work with. Really small amounts, but I finally managed to synthesize some. Again, not very much. I have to keep it shielded, of course."

"Of course."

"In a vacuum flask dispenser. A small electromagnetic cage might be even safer. I'm not sure. This kind of research is like groping in the dark . . ."

The interview had gone extremely well so far. Superficially, that is. On any other level it had gone preposterously, and Jim hardly knew what to do. He was a death-guide, not an abnormal psychiatrist — though he knew enough psychiatry to realize that Weinberger was definitely paranoid. And no House book covered such a case, for drugs, not guidance, helped the dying of the incurably insane.

Paranoid, yes. Weinberger had set up a self-consistent system based on the most outrageous of premises — a blend of persecution, private knowledge of The Truth (which nobody else knew), and a supposedly practical plan for proving the equivalent of day being night, or light being darkness. All because he was dying.

No, that couldn't be the reason. Weinberger had started on this mad course a whole decade ago . . .

Mad. And Jim had to guide him, notwithstanding, because the man in his madness had murdered Norman Harper and now he was too important simply to be drugged towards a peaceful death.

Somehow Weinberger's duties in the House of Death a decade ago must have unbalanced his mind. His mind had flipped into a new and unique configuration of beliefs utterly at odds with every-

36

thing taught and known in this country.

"How did you first discover all this? What set you on the trail?"

"I sat with a lot of my clients right through euthanasia. As they began to fade out — as the EEG began to pick up the pre-death 'thanatos' rhythm — well, I began to see something in the room. Only, I couldn't ever quite see it. I couldn't get a direct look. It was as though it was out of the corner of my eye."

'Out of the corner of your mind's eye,' thought Jim.

"No one else saw it?"

"Oh believe me, I was cautious about asking! I dropped a few hints — 'Is there a mosquito in the room?' 'Is there a moth in here?'— but I didn't want *that* on my records. Then I began seeing it all the time, while people were about to die. Almost seeing it, but never quite. It was there, though. It needed bringing out — like computer enhancement of a photograph. Yeah, it needed focusing. Then one day I happened to be present when there was an accident on the Beadway. Somehow an empty pod got detached. It fell right down and crushed one fellow and badly injured another. It nearly got me! And I wish it had! The first fellow died immediately, and I didn't see anything beside him. But the other fellow lingered on for five or ten minutes. The ambulance was delayed. And I saw this *thing* arrive — the same thing that I saw in the euthanasia room. I almost saw it."

So Weinberger had decided that he was the Galileo of Death . . . But where was his telescope, to see the mountains of the Moon? There couldn't be one.

"What did you plan to do with this corpse-sweat, as you call it? What was the big scheme, which the crab aborted?"

Oddly, Weinberger seemed to appreciate the almost brutal thrust of Jim's question. He was not quite as protective of his fantasy as Jim had imagined.

"Oh, how we hid ourselves from death in the old days! How we sheltered! What a wealth of resources we poured into shelters, once! Nuke shelters, right?"

"They're still okay for growing mushrooms in."

"But there's another sort of hide, Jim." Weinberger glanced up at the dead camera, mounted under the ceiling. "That's the photographer's hide — to snap the bird of death on the wing. I wasn't just going to build a tripwire camera, though. Oh no, I was a good deal more ambitious than that! I was going to build a cage — to trap that bird and hold it. I know how to do it, Jim. I got started, too. I almost finished. I can build . . . a cage for Death.''

A Cage for Death.

''You'll have to give me time to think about that one, Nathan.''

''Be my guest,'' said Weinberger smugly — smug in the certainty that Jim could never accept the notion?

Obviously, if Jim resisted it, this would only serve to reinforce Weinberger's fantasy. On the other hand, if Jim encouraged it much further at this moment, it might well bloom hysterically — giving Weinberger a massive set-back.

''It's a lot to take in at once.''

''Oh, it *is*.''

Too, Weinberger might feel that he had shown his whole hand prematurely. Then he would resent Jim bitterly.

''I'd rather like to check the literature for anything on the death pheromone.''

''You won't find a thing. I never did. I had to figure it all out myself.''

''There could have been some hint, some minor insight, that cropped up since you left the House. Something that didn't warrant announcing or publicising because it couldn't be properly demonstrated. There may be a record of it in Central Data.''

''Do you honestly imagine anybody else even *guessing* there was a pheromone to look for?''

''I think it's unlikely.''

''I'll tell you why you won't find anything new. It's rather important to decide the precise time of death, right? That's why you monitor the 'thanatos' rhythm — which *I'd* say is linked to the pheromone output, but I don't have the equipment to prove it . . . If anyone else had found out about the pheromone, you'd all be using that method routinely now! All it requires is a chemi-sniffer, sensitive to one part per billion. I rejigged one of the industrial ones — dead easy.'' Weinberger grinned triumphantly.

''Since you do know how to use this method, wouldn't it have been a nice idea to share your discovery with the Houses?''

''What? So that Death could feed on the dying even more efficiently? You must be joking. There's only one use that I'd see the pheromone method put to. That's as bait —''

"In a cage. For Death."

"Right. Tell the Houses? Goodness me."

'But you've told me,' thought Jim. Was Weinberger just too crazy to care, now? Or too bitterly disappointed? Or did he feel a need to *confess*? Yes, that was it, decided Jim. Weinberger needed to confess. It was good to confess. And Jim was someone whom he felt he could safely confess to.

"Even so, I'll check the literature. You never know."

"Oh, *I* do. It's you who don't know."

In common with everybody else.

SEVEN

JIM RETURNED TO his room right away and switched on the TV set. Dialling Central Data over the telephone link, he added his guide code in case he was seeking restricted information.

He regularly used his guide code to call up taboo literature featuring death. To begin with, this had simply been part of his training. Later, to guide difficult clients in Gracchus he had occasionally sought material for way-out therapy from this source. And, yes, for his own interest. He supposed that most guides did the same.

Outside the Houses of Death nobody seemed to regret the missing literature or object to the computer-adjusted versions. Yet Jim wondered whether some people actually volunteered as guides out of purely aesthetic motives, just to gain access to morbid, forbidden texts. In medieval times only inquisitors — or whatever they were called — could be trusted to read books on the *Index Expurgatorius*. Perhaps that was why the keenest minds had tended to end up in the old Church . . .

If such cupboard dilettantes tried to become guides these days, surely their hypno-analysis should screen them out. Those supposed 'aesthetic' motives would actually be wickedly erotic ones — for the only real pornography was violence and its counterpart, the dread of death.

'My record's reasonably clean,' he thought sadly, 'except for Mike's death in Gracchus. Was that really my fault? I merely overlooked the fact that he was actually dying, not just pretending to be.' A very fine distinction.

'Yes, it *was* my fault — as much as his, and he's not here to blame. Someone who really knew how to read the thanatos rhythms should have been on hand.'

Poor old Mike: with his red hair, now turned to ash, and his impish chuckle, and his yearning for the beyond, where he had arrived — or not arrived — so unexpectedly . . .

Despite his slight unfamiliarity with the technical medical index Jim was fairly sure within ten minutes that nothing whatever was known about a 'pheromone of death'. To be positive, he typed instructions for a 'clever search' on the touch-pad atop the TV set.

This kind of computer search was not so much clever as painstaking — and time-taking. A further ten minutes passed before the screen flashed for Jim's attention. The upshot of the search was precisely one item of computer graffiti, which some sick-minded enemy of the Houses must have programmed into the system once.

'DEATH STINKS,' read the screen.

For a moment Jim wondered whether Nathan Weinberger could somehow be responsible.

Hardly! Weinberger would have typed in, 'DYING PEOPLE STINK.' Weinberger had said that he saw Death out of the corner of his eye, not that he smelled it out of the side of his nose. Presumably Death itself was odourless.

Jim queried the touch-pad.

'NO FURTHER RECORD.'

He cleared the screen. Naturally there was nothing about a pheromone of death; for the simple reason that there wasn't one.

Jim paced. After a while the vista of Egremont beyond the sharp leaves and blood flowers reminded him that he ought to visit the Peace Office — the Octagon, as they called it here — to register. His schedule for these first few days was flexible — apart from the Weinberger affair — to let him find his bearings and fit in chores like this.

While he was down at the Octagon, perhaps he should ask a few discreet questions about Weinberger? Without, of course, implying that the House needed any advice . . .

He decided to catch some lunch on the way there. A visit to the fabled Three Spires Restaurant, perhaps? No — he wanted to save that experience up.

* * *

40

After walking for fifteen minutes, he chose a small sandwich bar. Half a dozen pine stools lined the counter, and there were just two tables. A couple of middle-aged men sat at one of these, over beers, saying nothing at all to each other, which was perhaps their most intimate way of communicating. Four women were munching doughnuts and drinking coffee at the other. The bar itself was decorated with resort pennants. Either its owner was privileged to travel, which seemed unlikely, or else he was a collector of such ephemera. Perhaps he had simply bought the pennants as a job lot from some shop furnisher.

Only two stools were vacant at the bar. Jim slipped in between a fat, bearded negro, and a bald old fellow with unusually large ears. Jim glanced at the old man, amused. As his frame had shrunk with age, so had his ears grown. His card must be coming up soon at the Census Office. Perhaps he had grown those ears to alert him to that moment, Jim thought whimsically.

He ordered smoked ham on rye and a small beer from the lady of the house, who was wearing what she perhaps thought of as a smart chiffon and lace blouse; unfortunately it looked more like part of a nightdress.

Inevitably, now that a guide had arrived, talk at the bar turned to the topic of the murder.

The negro was first in.

"So you're a guide, eh? You didn't do much guiding of that berserker up at the House yesterday."

"We do our best," said Jim evenly. "There was a time when an incident of that sort was so *ordinary* you wouldn't even have mentioned it. What kind of world was that?"

"Oh, a world on the skids. I guess we're just animals with brains too big for our own good. But now the animal trainers are in charge, right? So how did that nut get out of his cage?"

Jim sipped beer.

"He was the exception that proves the rule."

The old fellow's head swung round, as though operated by the crinkled dishes of his ears.

"Do you know what that saying really means, guide? What it means is, that the exception *tests* the rule — to see if it's okay, to see if it's worth anything. Or if it's just a phoney rule. That's the real meaning — the old meaning — and I'm sticking by it. And when my time comes I'm sticking by what I know. Like, for instance, death is shit."

"Charlie," said the nightdress lady sharply. "The work of the Houses is a blessing."

"If some people feel as Charlie does, it's understandable," said Jim.

"Oh, you're such an understanding lot up there! Understand a man to death, you will."

The negro laughed. "Well, nobody could ever understand you, Charlie! You belong in some other world."

"And they'll make darn sure they send me there."

"They daren't send *you* anywhere. Guiding you would be like trying to guide a bull through a china shop. By the ear!"

"You've had one too many, Charlie," said the lady.

"I have *not*." Charlie continued to sit defiantly, taking root in his stool.

The negro nudged Jim in the ribs. "Anyway, apart from this old fossil we're all on your side. It's just that you let the side down a bit yesterday, hey? It's like our best player missing the catch. The other side won that one: the old enemy of us all. The enemy of my kids. And yours."

"Right." Jim bit into his sandwich.

"But you guides don't have kids, do you? You must get kind of lonely."

Still chewing, Jim said, "There are compensations. Friends." (Such as Mike Mullen . . .?) "The sense that you're healing the world. And bringing people peace and joy. Fulfilling them."

"How about lady guides?" asked Charlie wickedly. "I hope *I* get one of those. She'll have to persuade me . . . quite touchingly."

"You're being disgusting," said the nightdress lady. She leaned across the bar, squashing her breasts tight against the chiffon. "And you guides retire earlier than most other people — some of whom we could quite well do without! I think you're saints."

"Thanks," said Jim. He raised his glass to her. "We're just people, as you see."

"And people like to have a drink. It's so *good* to see you here." She beamed. "Your next beer's for free. You might say it's on the House."

"And you're very welcome up at the House, any time there's a seminar," said Jim chivalrously. "Even if we do only serve coffee."

"Yeah, we saw Barnes saying how we should go up there more often," remarked the negro. "Is that what you're doing in town? Delivering invitations?"

"Me? I'm off to the Octagon, to register. I just arrived in Egremont yesterday."

The negro looked crestfallen. "And here's me sounding off at you about what happened! Damn it all, I'm sorry. What's your name?"

"Jim."

"Mine's Alec. *I'll* buy the next one."

With four beers under his skin, Jim carried on to the Octagon.

As he walked across the gravel courtyard towards the grand portico, he ran his hand through one of the standard bay trees, rattling the leaves, a few of which fell off. The marble statues watched him blankly.

Along the architrave ran the gilded inscription: PAX VOBISCUM — 'Peace Be With You.' Composing himself, he hoped that his face was not too flushed. He mounted the wide stone steps between the fluted pillars. Glass doors whispered apart.

Registration only took a few moments. A white-uniformed woman handled it at the front desk. She had short black hair, except where she had trained long lacquered sweeps down past her cheekbones to her jaw, so that she seemed to be wearing an ancient Roman helmet.

When she handed back Jim's code-card, he said, "There's one other thing. I'm the person who's guiding Norman Harper's murderer."

"You have my sympathy."

"Thanks. But apart from that I thought that someone from here might have checked into the man's background . . ."

"Ah, you're having difficulties?"

"I wouldn't say that."

"But you'd like to compare notes?"

"Sort of. Well, not exactly *compare* — I can't reveal anything about my client."

"We have our rules too, Mr Todhunter. Still, I'll phone around.

43

No, wait a minute: if I remember, Officer Bekker did some checking.''

A few minutes later, a messenger was leading Jim up a wide, circling marble staircase and along a corridor to Bekker's office.

Bekker sat at his desk, which was partly data terminal, beneath a frosted glass window. He was checking a printout. A framed aerial blow-up of the Egremont valley hung on the wall, next to a large map studded with coloured pins.

Jim identified himself.

Bekker was about forty years old, with hair the colour of hay and a slight moustache. He had a small wart on one cheek. He looked vaguely familiar.

"Wasn't it you I gave the gun to?"

"If you're the same guy who gave it to me, then I'm the one. Do you want it back now?" Bekker grinned.

"I wanted to know whether you'd visited Nathan Weinberger's apartment.''

"Sure.''

"Did you find anything . . . interesting?"

"It depends what you mean by interesting. There wasn't any cache of guns and bullets, which is what I was mainly looking for. But the furnishings were pretty weird. He'd built the craziest bed for himself: like a water-bed crossed with a four-poster. You'd have to see it for yourself! Instead of curtains and awnings, it had this gilded cage around it with a little door. He had five — count 'em, five — scene-screens stacked against the wall. What that must have cost! And electronic stuff, cameras, tools, some chemical equipment. But he hadn't stolen any of it. Bought it all. Spent every penny that came in — so his credit balance was nearly nil. Good worker, though. But he kept to himself.''

"What do you think he was up to, buying things like that?"

"Think? I *know*. He was fixing up an electronic harem for himself. He was going to feed sex tapes into those screens, and he was going to lie there on his water bed peeping through that naughty harem grille. I didn't find any tapes, but I did find a stack of nudie magazines. Quite a big stack. Which hardly concerns me, so long as he was peaceful — and I guess you couldn't get more peaceful than that! But there were a couple of tiny little cameras too, for filming what went on on that bed — and I'm sure it wouldn't be himself he was planning on filming. I'd say he was planning on luring little boys up there. Little girls too, maybe. In which case it would certainly have become my business. It's a good thing the Hospital retired him; or we'd have had to do it. Me, I prefer a different sort of photography." Bekker waved at the blow-up of the valley. "I took that picture myself."

"Very impressive."

"It's got a whole lot of detail in it. There's no blurring."

"And all that, er, electronic harem stuff is still in his apartment?"

"Where else? Public Disposal sealed the apartment on the day he retired. It stays that way till he dies, then they clear it and re-allocate."

"I just wondered if you'd removed anything — by way of evidence?"

"Evidence of what? A plan for sexual entrapment of minors? That's irrelevant now. Personally I think this courtesy of sealing somebody's place and holding it in limbo for weeks on end is stupid. Kick it off the statute book, I say. It's wasteful. It's point-less. No one who retires is going to be returning to his old haunts."

"It's important psychologically."

"Oh well, you know more about that than I do. Anyhow, I hope I've been some help. Now you know why he fired the gun. He had a sexual screw loose. Probably he couldn't cut the mustard any longer. Then he lost control of his harem before he could even open it to the junior public. All he could fire off was a gun."

Jim got up to leave.

"Thanks for your help, Mr Bekker."

"Give my best to Noel," said Bekker, by way of goodbye.

"Noel? Oh, you mean Resnick?"

Bekker stared at Jim. "Didn't Noel Resnick send you? Didn't he suggest you see me?"

"No, I just came. I had to register, you see, so I asked the officer downstairs . . ."

"Well, fancy that," said Bekker. "What a subtle guide you must be — though *I* don't presume to tread on *your* terrain!"

"I'm sorry if I gave the wrong impression."

"Think nothing of it. Yes, an ideal guide for Mr Weinberger! Dark horses, both of you."

EIGHT

WHEN JIM CALLED on Weinberger the next morning, it was obvious that the dying man did not intend to be the first to raise the matter of death pheromones or a cage for Death. So Jim did not rush in to these topics, either — and this seemed to please Weinberger. Perhaps it confirmed his opinion that Jim was just like all the others. Or maybe Weinberger thought that he had thrown Jim off the scent?

After what Bekker had told him, Jim had his reservations about the genuineness of any plan to entrap Death. Weinberger would presume that the Peace Office had searched his apartment. His story about the intended use of the cage might be nothing more than a smokescreen, to hide his shame and guilt at the actual fetishistic, erotic purpose he had in mind.

Yes indeed, fetishism and frustration might easily account for his pouring all his energy and money into building the 'electronic harem'. Weinberger had become obsessed, fixated. Yet his fixation had little to do with death — except maybe with the little death of orgasm, something that had perhaps withered from his life except in certain specialised circumstances. If, indeed, it had ever blossomed much at all! He *was* rather an ugly man.

"You must have been lonely these last ten years?" suggested Jim. "I mean, with all you had to do, and how much it must have cost and everything. It couldn't have left much over for enjoyment."

"Don't worry about me. I could afford a drink now and then."

"So you had drinking buddies?"

"One or two."

"But no women friends."

"You mean no sex?" Weinberger laughed. "I've lived in a House. I know what a hotbed this place feels like now and then

46

— to some people. But I'm a bit different. If I went to bed casually with a woman I'd half fall in love with her. I know it! I'm too damn sentimental that way. You mightn't believe it, but it's a fact. And how could I ever possibly let myself love anyone, knowing as I do that the most loving, kindest thing I could possibly do would be . . . kill her, unexpectedly?

"To kill my love," he repeated softly, "to cheat Death out of her."

'Sick,' thought Jim. He kept the thought from registering on his face.

Perhaps Weinberger's vacuum flask dispenser actually contained *sexual* pheromones? Perhaps he thought that he could turn himself on thus, together with whoever else he could wheedle into his apartment! It was the modern version of drenching a bed with perfume . . .

And yet . . . if Weinberger was telling the truth about his motive in building the cage, it would follow logically that anyone whom he really loved ought to die suddenly and unexpectedly. So, not having anyone to love, having indeed denied himself the chance, he had killed Norman Harper instead — the beloved of many people. Maybe that was the closest he could come to his wish.

Anyone could own a pile of nudie magazines, if they had vowed themselves to celibacy. (But not to continence.)

"I'll reserve judgement on that one," said Jim.

"Take your time," said Weinberger bitterly. "You can't take mine — I haven't any left to spare."

Early that Friday evening six staff members boarded an electric minibus to purr northwards through Egremont to Lake Tulane.

Alice Huron drove. Noel Resnick sat next to her. Behind were Jim and Marta Bettijohn, Lama Ananda, and Mary-Ann Sczepanski, who had been Weinberger's guide before the débâcle.

Mary-Ann wore girlish blond pigtails, though she looked to be in her early forties. Slim and trim and slight, and full of nervous energy, she was constantly looking this way and that as though this was her first glimpse of the town. All was a perpetual wonder to her, to be greeted with a quick smile — as, no doubt, she would greet death when her time came to retire. Maybe she was doing this to avoid concentrating on Jim, who had taken over her role with

Weinberger? He sensed no jealousy or resentment, though. But she wasn't going to volunteer to mention Weinberger. It would be a breach of House etiquette. Yet breaches occurred, as Jim well knew — there had been a breach big enough to drive this minibus through the other day in Resnick's office. Excused, no doubt, by the extraordinary circumstances.

Perhaps Mary-Ann wasn't very good at dealing with the extraordinary. So, instead, she exalted the familiar. Weinberger had easily fooled her. Weinberger was way outside of her competence.

And so Jim, too, admired the town.

The sun was beginning to set when they arrived by the lake. Egremont in its valley was a bowl of shadow, criss-crossed by faint pearly beads of light, but the encircling hills remained brightly lit, with shadows sharp and black. A mercury river ran westward over the lake. A thousand semaphore signals from the crests of waves dazzled their eyes. Most of the yachts had already returned to their moorings and boathouses around the shore. The deep blue sky was whisped with high cirrus clouds — white in the east, thin veins of blood in the west. It was fair weather now, and the breeze was only moderate, yet a depression was moving in.

Alice Huron steered the minibus along a cinder track to a chalet. Another minibus was already parked there. Jim recognized the operatic figure of Claudio Menotti amidst a small group of people whom he did not yet know, but soon would. Two attendants from the House had already fired the hibachi and loaded a log table with glasses and chilled wine bottles, under the bunchy spread of a Corsican pine. Junipers grew along the gravel shoreline.

Soon Jim was being toasted by Noel Resnick, rather floridly.

After the toast Resnick drew Jim aside, down through the junipers to the stony shore.

"How's it going, then?"

How was *what* going? Jim's adjustment to Egremont after his life in the city? Or the Weinberger affair?

Not one to fudge an issue — as he believed that Mary-Ann might well have fudged one previously, with all her sweet enthusiasm — Jim opted for the second interpretation.

"I'm making good contact with Nathan. That part's fine. But the man has some pretty fierce obsessions. He certainly isn't going to bow out gracefully until he has a chance to work them through. He has to purge himself of the causes of the murder.''

This was, perhaps, an optimistic assessment.

"Could you be a bit more specific?"

"Not at this stage, if you don't mind. I might still be getting a partial picture. I might distort his view of things if I tried to put it into words so soon. I'd certainly distort my own view of him."

"Quite right, Jim. But he hasn't got *much* time left. He mustn't . . . simply die."

"Unredeemed? Don't worry, we've got several weeks — and with someone really listening to his point of view . . ."

"And playing along with it? He'll hang on?"

"I'm sure he will."

"Is it wise to play along with major delusions?"

"Sometimes we play along with the delusion of an afterlife," said Jim.

"That isn't *his* delusion . . . is it?"

"It might be involved. I'm not sure yet."

"A dying person must face the truth of death."

"But to resist Nathan's delusions at this stage would be to alienate him. It would harden his shell. He'd retreat." And at that very moment Jim made up his mind about Weinberger's abandoned deathtrap. The cage had never been intended as a sexual playpen at all. It was precisely what Weinberger said it was. And Jim made up his mind, too, about what he would do with it.

"I'm going to play along with Weinberger all the way. By doing that he'll realize that the way leads nowhere. He'll turn aside, on to the true path."

"I really hope so. I hope he can appear in public, a little before the end, as . . . a changed person." Resnick waggled his fingers. "We'd be discreet. He wouldn't be traumatised or set back. It's because of what he did, and the echoes he set up — do you see? I know it's unusual. But if some clients can share their death experience in seminars, well, we'll hold a small public ceremony, of reconciliation, eh? In effect, he'll *become* Norman Harper. He'll take Norman's place. That'll cancel out the tragedy."

"We're still some way off that happy day."

"Okay, Jim, handle it any way you like. You have *carte blanche* from me. Just *get* Weinberger there. This is important. Norman

49

was a major figure, and for him to be cheated of his death by somebody in our care . . ."

Resnick waved his hand, emphasizing a whole lake of importance. The mercury river had withdrawn into the sun, which was about to slip behind a hill. Looking across the lake, Jim thought of the intense feeling of identification, of oceanic unity, which he had experienced when he drowned. Once, in Gracchus during their mimicry of the death encounter, he had recaptured that blissful feeling.

'Shall I really help Nathan build a cage for Death?' he wondered. There was an odd and slightly ugly fascination in the notion. It was an absurdity, rather as though a modern chemist should decide to build alchemical apparatus to transmute lead into gold. It was the direct opposite of everything the Houses stood for.

'When Nathan catches nothing in it, obviously we'll be home and dry. Still . . .

'I'm treading on eggs,' he thought. And, for some perverse reason — perhaps because Resnick was so fatuously and *politically* anxious to conclude this sorry episode serenely — 'I want to.'

'They robbed *me* of something too,' thought Jim. 'They robbed me of the chance of navigating the Ocean of Unity, when Mike Mullen imitated death all too well in Gracchus, and genuinely died . . .'

Should he convey Officer Bekker's greetings to Resnick?

"I'd like you to take on a few other cases," went on Resnick, before Jim had time to decide. "There's a young kid — she's just eleven — who was transferred from the Hospital yesterday. They diagnosed leukaemia. The white blood-crab. Needs sympathy, but she's well-adjusted."

Jim nodded.

"And a middle-aged woman with severe heart disease. She'll be glad to go. And a farmer who developed multiple sclerosis. He'll be retiring. No problem. Three or four others, too, including a couple of voluntary retirements — you won't have any trouble there. So you'll still be able to *focus* upon Weinberger."

"I'll focus on them all," said Jim firmly. "Everybody's death is equally precious."

"Of course."

"Chow time!" called a cheery voice. Marta Bettijohn came

bustling through the junipers. "You mustn't let your trout get cold!"

Both Mary-Ann and Alice Huron became tipsy later on, largely because Noel Resnick freshened their drinks in a lordly manner.

By now the cirrus clouds were thickening in a darkening sky. The air grew humid. The breeze was freshening to a wind from off the water. Battery lamps were brought from the chalet and switched on.

The two women, one tall, one small, linked arms, confusing their glasses.

" 'The day is over, perfect day,' " Alice sang out in a maudlin way. She blinked down at Mary-Ann; perhaps there were tears in her eyes.

Perhaps there were tears, too — of sentiment — in Mary-Ann's.

" 'Now the day is over,' " Mary-Ann recited, but then she forgot, or swung off course. Her voice was slurred. Glancing up at the sky, where dark horses' manes blew out below the first cold prickling stars, she found confused inspiration. "Now the day is over, nightmares drawing nigh . . ." She giggled.

A few spots of rain struck the party, and hissed on the hibachi. The party broke up.

Only when a dozen or more people had crowded into the one minibus and it was moving off with Marta Bettijohn at the wheel beside him, did Jim realize that Resnick and the other minibus — and the two tipsy women — had stayed behind. As their own minibus departed, lights blinked on in the chalet then cut down to chinks as shutters were closed against the storm which might soon break: against the hot stabbing electricity of the sky.

Crowding Jim's other side was Claudio Menotti, who hummed to himself more noisily than the electric motor. Jim leaned against Marta. He nodded back towards the chalet.

And quoted, humorously, " 'Too much in love with easeful death', eh, Marta?"

"I hate those morbid old poems," she said sharply. "I'm glad nobody spoils their minds with them any more."

"But didn't death produce good poetry?" asked Jim. He realized that he had gone too far; he must be rather drunk too.

51

NINE

"So how do you go about building a cage for Death, Nathan? I'm perfectly serious. I want to help you build one. I have to see this with my own eyes."

"Don't patronize *me*."

Jim had not expected instant gratitude. Deep down, Weinberger probably did not believe that his cage would work. Jim's instinct had been right: build the cage, use it, prove it useless — then Weinberger would be free of his delusion.

Weinberger had changed the scene in the wall screen. In one way, this was a bad sign. Dying people, who had accepted their death, tended to absorb themselves wholly in a single landscape of choice: a landscape, of course, without human characters or any living creatures, a landscape of eternal vegetative nature, or better still, pure ocean.

The new scene was arctic, as though its coldness might act to slow down the decay of Weinberger's body. Great white icebergs like mountainous teeth — molars and incisors — floated in blue fluoride waters. The scene was sterile and aseptic, and beautiful too. It also conveyed a certain frozen violence: of icy jaws, locked in a total stoppage of time. If those jaws were ever to move, what a grinding and crashing there would be! But they couldn't, and didn't. So all was serene. Which was, perhaps, a good sign.

"I am certainly *not* patronising you."

"No? Well, Mr Todhunter, let's just prove it, hmm?"

"I'll prove it one way, right now. I'll tell you a secret. Noel Resnick has given me absolute *carte blanche* to handle your case — so that you can work things through and see the light."

'The arctic light,' thought Jim. 'The everlasting stillness and silence of the ice wastes where nothing lives . . . (Untrue! Fish live there, and seals, and great whales . . . Do any equivalent creatures inhabit the realm of death? Is that what Nathan imagines?)'

"That's how I can go along with you. And equally, here's your chance, because I'm going to use that *carte blanche* to the full."

The sick man licked his lips. "They won't like it."

"They needn't know, particularly. Of course, we can't do it *here*. This room's unsuitable, what with attendants and nurses dropping in. I'll commandeer a spare room in the basement."

Weinberger's face drained of trust.

"I won't be fooled by a masquerade. Me locked up here, you in the basement — so you say."

"I'll take you down there along with me. I'll obey all your directions. Anything you want from outside, I'll fetch. Any other equipment you need, I'll get hold of somehow."

Jim stuck out his hand.

"Is it a deal?"

Weinberger's grip was surprisingly strong. It felt as though he was diverting all the remaining strength of his body into his right hand, in order to grasp something beyond Jim's own hand: something invisible, elusive and mighty.

Weinberger grinned. "You can't make deals with Death. But you can catch it, and clobber it."

"Whatever you say. And I *mean* that."

One week later, Jim stood in the blue-painted basement room with Weinberger, surveying the 'machine' which he had assembled according to the dying man's directions, and with his occasional assistance.

Apart from the cage and a pair of chairs, the room was bare. It was the same experimental room that Resnick had told him about. Soundproofing baffles scalloped and fluted the walls, so that being in here was like being in some large rectangular lung which breathed through silent, hidden air ducts.

The machine consisted of the waterbed which Bekker had described. Within its strong pine frame it was raised off the ground on rubber-buffered, insulated legs, and entirely surrounded by a delicate filigree Faraday cage which could block out any electromagnetic radiation from outside, or isolate any radiation arising from within. So much for the 'harem grille' notion! It occurred to Jim to wonder whether Weinberger had been sleeping inside the

53

Faraday cage for many months prior to his enforced retirement *with the current switched on* as a way of insulating and isolating himself from the power that he feared. Perhaps this had contributed in some obscure way to the onset of his illness!

Using the authority of the House to over-ride Public Disposal, and with a waiver signed by Weinberger, Jim had had no difficulty in entering Weinberger's former abode to remove whatever he chose.

With the aid of an attendant from the House he had also brought back the polarisable glass screens which Weinberger had told him he would find stacked in the bedroom, as he already knew from Bekker. These were actually adapted scene-screens. Bolted together around the sides and roof of the cage, these screens would no longer display illusions of African savannah or Amazonian forest. They acted instead either as a perfectly clear five-fold window, or else they could be rendered opaque. Then, from inside the cage, they became a maze of mirrors reflecting mirrors. So much for the sex tape idea! Though, of course, one could always readjust the screens . . .

A hooded optic fibre periscope allowed one to spy into the cage from outside while the glass walls were opaque. Two tiny automatic cameras were mounted on silver rods inside. A drip-feed led from a tiny vacuum flask, looking like a spout for feeding humming birds on the wing. This flask supposedly contained the 'corpse sweat' which Weinberger had synthesized like a home alchemist. Strapped beside this was an industrial chemi-sniffer, apparently rejigged to be sensitive to one part in a billion per volume of the pheromone.

Cannibalised by Jim from the neighbouring Hospital, and from the House, were other pieces of equipment that had been beyond Weinberger's means. Medi-sensors were taped across the surface of the waterbed, connected to vital signs monitors outside. A skull-cap sensitive to the 'thanatos' brain rhythm of the 'death plateau' — to be worn by the occupant of the bed — was linked with an oscilloscope outside. From outside, too, a remote-controlled stimulant syringe could be operated.

To Jim's eyes Weinberger's machine looked like an old piece of Dada art, something reminiscent of Marcel Duchamp's *Great Glass*: a machine for pursuing an enigma in the realm of the irrational, of the wholly imaginary. It was a machine for hunting a

Snark. It was an insane satire, translated into rubber and steel, wire, glass and wood, on the techniques of adjustment to the Inevitable which was life's fulfilment, not its catastrophe or betrayal.

'Mozart wrote all his symphonies, didn't he?' thought Jim. 'Which unwritten ones did he fail to write?' And yet, and yet . . .

But there was nothing absurd about the machine to Weinberger. He quite glowed to see it all assembled, with the extra medical facilities to which he could never have gained access. In a sense, Jim realized, Weinberger was indeed approaching the culmination of his life, in the shape of this 'machine'. Jim had been quite right to play along with the man's fantasies. Here was Weinberger's vision of death, and quite soon Weinberger was going to enter into it and become one with it.

The only snag was that the machine would do nothing. Nothing at all. Merely purr, or hiss, or crackle, and render itself opaque, and drip minute amounts of *something* into the air within.

Yet that, too, would be excellent. 'Look, Nathan, it doesn't hurt. There isn't anything. Death is nothing.'

"I built little pilot models, you know," confided Weinberger. "Prototype death-traps, to catch whatever vectored in on the pheromone. But they didn't work. Death wasn't fooled. Obviously there had to be an actual dying body there. So I bought some rabbits —"

"You should be ashamed of yourself. That was what was so *sick* about medicine in the old days: the slaughter, the mutilation, the agony of so many poor creatures so that people could keep alive for five minutes longer! It was just another symptom of our whole death sickness, which would have burnt the planet bare."

"Okay, I know the spiel too. And I *was* disgusted, believe me. It seemed as if I was *sacrificing* to Death."

It began with rabbits. It ended up with Norman Harper.

Weinberger spread his hands placatingly.

"No result. Then I got the idea that maybe the death of animals and the death of people is different in essence . . ."

"That's the old Catholic doctrine that animals have no souls. The idea that animals are automatic objects. *That* was another part of the whole sickness — the disrespect."

"Sure. Now nothing has a soul, so everything is holy."

To which Jim said nothing. Afterlife studies necessarily implied that something outlasted death, even if it wasn't a bundle of memories and personality in the old sense of a soul . . . And certainly the radiant unity that Jim had experienced when he drowned must be classed as holy.

Weinberger frowned.

"It appears to be ready . . ." Jim said.

Like a virgin actor who had forgotten his lines, Weinberger froze. He stalled.

"Could we make a start tomorrow?" he asked apologetically. "We've worked damn hard today."

Jim smiled sympathetically.

"Would you rather I lay down in it instead of you?"

Abruptly, Weinberger grinned back. "Then I release the non-existent whiff of cyanide gas? To zap *your* death? Ah, there's nothing like that in my machine! Maybe there ought to be."

Jim pressed home.

"Is that why you had the gun? Was it to shoot Death with when it came into your cage? But you'd only smash the glass, and let it out. What did you have in that gun: silver bullets?"

"It was an old . . . souvenir. The gun."

And maybe that was why Weinberger had hung on to it. To shoot Death. Death was the mugger who broke into your apartment. Death was the rapist, who took you by force. At least, in the old way of looking at it.

"You can try it for size if you like," Weinberger offered. He was in a 'bargaining' mode, thought Jim. "Go ahead — I'm not proprietorial. This'll be a famous bed soon. Far more famous than any of your beds where Good Queen Bess or Abraham Lincoln slept."

"Well, thanks but no thanks."

"If I *could* equip it with cyanide gas . . . I really wonder whether I'd be killing Death in general, or just the personal death of whoever was in the machine?"

"A whole lot of people die every hour, Nathan. They even die *simultaneously*. Even if this Death of yours skipped around at the speed of light —"

"Okay, okay. But Death might be general *and* particular. If I kill the particular death — if I zap the bullet with this person's own special name on it, right out of the way, swat it, squash it, vaporise it! — would this person," and here Weinberger's hand drifted over the imaginary contours of his subject 'volunteer', as sensuously — thought Jim — as some fantasizing soldier in the old days of war, stuck in a jungle hundreds of miles from a brothel, "would this person *live for ever*? Would I have invented an immortality treatment, here in the midst of the House of Death? That would be one hell of an irony!"

"It would certainly be a way of getting people to volunteer," allowed Jim. "Roll up, roll up! Climb into Weinberger's Death Cage and he'll make thee immortal with a hiss . . . of cyanide gas. Ah, but you're forgetting something, my friend. You'd kill the person, that way, before you nailed his death. Baby and the bathwater, Nathan. Baby and the bathwater!"

Weinberger looked crestfallen, as though he had seriously considered the possibility. As perhaps he had. Jim was now doubly sure that the gun had been kept hidden from long ago with just some such plan in mind. Instead of which, Weinberger had used it to shoot Norman Harper, to save the poet — absurdly — from falling into the clutches of Death . . .

"With these medi-sensors and the 'thanatos' screen hooked in," said Jim, "we need somebody on hand who's qualified in using the apparatus." He wanted a witness, for his own protection. He also wished most dearly to avoid a repetition of what had happened in Gracchus.

Weinberger nodded.

"I took the liberty of having a word with Claudio Menotti — our euthanaser."

"I know who *he* is. He was on the platform at the ceremony. Oh boy, was he looking forward to his duties! Surely you didn't tell him about —?"

"*Of course* I didn't. I simply asked to borrow one of his assistants to keep an eye on certain medical equipment."

Weinberger's face showed a mixture of intense relief, and almost paranoid suspicion. Relief, because the equivalent of a dental appointment for a deep filling was now certainly postponed —

"Oh, so we couldn't have got started this afternoon in any case?"

And suspicion: that somehow the cage might be transformed without his knowledge into a euthanasia machine, which he would enter unwittingly.

To allay the suspicion, Jim said quickly, "Noel Resnick told me he wanted you to make a public appearance before the end. To atone. I think we can safely put that off for a while, eh?"

Weinberger smiled happily. His cage was safe. He was safe too — except from the Death which he hoped to lure into the cage, to trap.

"The assistant's called Sally Costello. She won't know what's *really* going on. I put it to Menotti that this is a special therapy experiment sanctioned by Resnick. Which, actually, it is."

Weinberger nodded. Jim felt sure that the man would guide himself to his own good death with hardly a guiding touch on his arm after his flirtation with this preposterous apparatus.

"We'll set the trap tomorrow?"

"Just one tiny point," said Jim. "Are you *sure* that you can ape the death state satisfactorily, without actually dying?"

He knew by now that Weinberger had also been deeply interested, while a guide, in trance states which closely approximated the actual journey into death. This discovery had forged something of a bond between the two men during the past week, though Nathan had shown no interest as yet in the oceanic unity that could be achieved that way. Weinberger rode to battle: to wage war, not peace. And yet, while helping to assemble the machine, Jim had become increasingly aware of a curious similarity between its supposed purpose and that of the sensory deprivation tank which he and Mike Mullen had built back in Gracchus, to investigate the death-trance using bio-feedback from the 'thanatos' rhythm.

Jim wondered how Weinberger could possibly achieve the peace of mind necessary to induce the death-trance — though Nathan had assured him that he would be able to. The benefits of Weinberger's achieving this state, for whatever purpose, should be considerable — while the risk of going too far into death ought certainly to be minimised by Nathan's core of anger. In his machine, Weinberger would in fact be studying the art of genuine dying, as an unintentional byproduct. When the cage produced no other result, this at least would remain as a boon to the dying man. So actually Jim had been telling the honest truth to Claudio Menotti when he described the whole business as experimental therapy.

Weinberger gripped Jim by the arm. "What do you mean — without actually dying?"

"It's an occupational hazard of death-mimicry," he said lightly, his tone entirely belying the sorrow and deprivation that he felt just then. "I lost a dear friend. In Gracchus. He was called Mike Mullen. He mimicked death not wisely but too well. And went. That's why the Gracchus House closed down its afterlife studies. That's how I got transferred out here."

"Fellow, I won't die. Not on this bed, at any rate! Oh no!" Weinberger swung Jim round, and stared into his face. "I know how you'd hate to lose me before my time."

Releasing Jim, he touched a lever on the medi-console, and the stimulant syringe twitched forward inside the cage. Encountering no obstacle of flesh, it did not discharge its drug.

Weinberger rubbed his hands together.

"This is a *good* set-up," he said affectionately. "It's better than any I could have designed myself, with all these extras. You're right — it would have been risky all alone in my apartment. Well, not alone — I'd have had a friend keep watch. One of my buddies. That's why the periscope's here. But would he have been on the ball? No, I need qualified observers. How odd," he smiled, "that Death should be trapped and trounced in his own House. Yet how appropriate!"

Poor man, thought Jim. Poor deluded man. At least, on that waterbed, he could learn to float his way out on to the ocean of unity.

Jim escorted Weinberger back to his room, then he went to guide his other charges elsewhere in the House.

TEN

SALLY COSTELLO WAS a chunky young woman with cascades of dark curly hair. She favoured a loose, robe-like style of dress, with her arms bare to the shoulders and several serpentine bracelets pressing her flesh. Hers was a moon face, with prominent cheeks which were somewhat pocked beneath a layer of powder. Jim imagined dust drifting into little meteor craters up on the dead world — though there was little that was dead about Sally Costello, aside from her job as Menotti's assistant. She beamed frequently, as a natural function of the prominence of her cheeks. Her eyes twinkled. Her robe swirled. She tossed her curls. Jim wondered a little at her operatic role in her duet with Menotti. She reminded him of Mary-Ann Sczepanski, but she was younger and fleshier.

She ran her hands over the medi-console, familiarising herself, like a musician who sees an instrument but does not really know it till she touches it. She glanced through the glass walls which boxed the golden cage about, and beamed.

It was a mousetrap, thought Jim, with Weinberger soon to be laid out as the bait, synthetically scented with the gorgonzola of death — a smell which neither Jim nor Sally Costello would be able to detect.

The 'bait' was dressed in brief shorts and a string vest. Thus the medi-sensors could read his status easily. In this kit Weinberger looked like a victim of starvation about to sprint the hundred metres. As he stood waiting he jiggled his gaunt limbs, as though to warm up.

"Let's get started," said Jim. He pulled back the glass wall from the cage door, which he unfastened. Weinberger crawled through into the Faraday cage, careful not to buckle any of the thin wire framework. Stretching himself out on the waterbed, he reached back to don the sticktight skullcap. For a short while the bed undulated sluggishly.

"Good hunting, Nathan."

Weinberger nodded. Composing himself, he shut his eyes. Having closed the door, Jim locked it with the gilt key which Weinberger had fastidiously included in his design, and slipped the thin key chain around his neck. Then he shut the glass panel.

He switched on the current to the cage at minimum power. It hummed faintly.

"Air recycling *on*," he said to himself.

"He looks like a scarecrow version of Snow White," called Sally Costello. Weinberger would hardly be able to hear her now. "But where's the poisoned apple?"

"Everywhere. In his guts, in his liver, in his spleen — metastasizing. Lodged all over."

"Oh. I suppose so." She went back to checking his vital signs

60

on the read-outs.

Inside that glassed-in golden cage Weinberger began to intone a monotonous, hypnotic refrain to himself in tune with the mild electric hum. As Jim watched the man's lips move, silently it seemed, he nodded approval. Weinberger was really quite adept at this technique.

Or had been, once. The mumbling went on for a long while, till the room seemed to have frozen in time. Sally's head, bowed over the console and hooding it in black ringlets, was that of a waxwork.

At last Weinberger raised a limp hand — it was barely a gesture at all — and Jim touched the button to opaque the glass walls.

A milky fastness confronted Jim. Weinberger and his golden cage had vanished from the world.

Jim bent to the periscope, resting his brow on the hood. Inside the cage, not even Weinberger's lips moved now. He was utterly still. In the pearly interior light he looked even more convincingly blanched and corpse-like. The mock-corpse lay beside a mirrored self, which lay beside another mirrored self . . . Toe to toe, and head to head with yet others. Each lay in its own frail gilded cage, the bars of which overlaid each other as bodies multiplied further and further till they faded out and there was nothing else to be seen but bars. Right now Weinberger's machine seemed like some device for cloning dead bodies. It was quite easy to lose one's centre of focus in there.

The descent into the death trance took the best part of an hour. Jim began to doubt whether Weinberger would ever achieve it. He felt sure that the man's subconscious was putting up resistance, and possibly part of his conscious mind too. Jim alternated periods of periscope watch with intervals of staring at the blank wall before him. The glass box was a great marble block now, impenetrably solid: a white kaaba. How could there be anyone inside it? But he looked down, and there was — and then the box was a mausoleum. He looked up again.

Suddenly Sally shook her hair free of her screen, breaking the spell. She tapped the screen with a chubby finger, squeezed by a large bronze ring which would never slide off until her flesh melted from her bones. Perhaps that was why she wore that ring and the squeezing bracelets.

"He's done it. Here's the start of the thanatos rhythm."

61

Jim hugged the periscope hood around his head, and only heard her voice.

"The other rhythms have flattened out now. It'll take four or five minutes before the thanatos wave is full enough to trip that drip-feed contraption."

"Ah . . . drip-feed is on now."

Jim sniffed reflectively, though he knew he would not be able to smell anything.

He focused on the point of the needle, waiting near Weinberger's bare calf to plunge a massive dose of stimulants into the man at Sally's command if the need arose. He kept his own hand on the squeeze-button which would multiply the power fed into the Faraday cage by fifty-fold. This should step up the power automatically when certain micro-electronic patterns appeared, about which Weinberger had not been entirely precise — perhaps he was hoping to claim a patent? — but Jim was a human back-up system able to exercise his own judgement.

Suddenly something flickered . . . into existence. A red thing — except that it was not really 'red' — appeared abruptly, perching upon Weinberger's chest.

It was like a bat, or like a giant moth. . . . It flickered: it seemed to dance in and out of existence. It had big glassy eyes — if they were eyes — as red as the rest of its body. And a cruel little beak. It wore sharp hooks on its veil-like wings — if they were wings — like the spurs of a fighting cock from the bygone years of cruelty. The thing seemed to be trying to reach the back of Weinberger's neck — its beak ducked forward, hen-like — but it kept hopping back to where his heartbeat was.

It was like various things, but what was it in itself? Despite his shock, Jim realized that he was only seeing what his eyes and brain *could* see, not necessarily what was actually there . . .

"Thanatos finale!" sang out Sally, oblivious to any of this. "Stimulating, *now*."

Jim squeezed his button at the same moment. But whatever micro-electronic gizmo Weinberger had included had already done its job. The cage crackled with fifty-fold insulation.

Simultaneously the needle slid into Weinberger's calf. Weinberger jerked like a galvanised frog, from the old time

62

of torture experiments.

He sat upright on the water-bier, his eyes wide open.

The red thing leapt away from him, flickering, phasing in, phasing out — more in than out. It hit the side of the cage and seemed to pass through the electrified filigree; and through the glass walls too.

But *no*. It passed through, yet not into the room which Jim and Sally shared. It passed through into one of the reflected doubles of the cage — *actually* into it, leaving no 'original' behind in the real cage.

Jim realized now that there had only ever been 'one' of it from the moment of its first appearance. In his initial shock at seeing it he had failed to understand this, though his brain had recorded the fact. *There had been no reflections.* No mirror duplicates. Many reflections there had been of Nathan Weinberger — but none of it. How could something which he could see with his eyes not have a reflection in a mirror? Perhaps . . . because it was indivisible. Nothing could double it — any more than a man could die twice. This weird characteristic made the creature seem more real than if it had possessed a hundred reflections: wherever it flew to, it existed *totally*. It was as though this creature had soaked up all potential reflections *into itself*, so that it could be seen fully — intensified — not just glimpsed out of the corner of one's eye. And that was precisely the magic, or the technology, of Weinberger's cage!

Circling outward from the real Nathan Weinberger, the red bat-moth beat from one phantom cage to the next. Yet the further it flew outward, the more golden bars got in the way. Very soon it was flying into a wall of thick syrup. It could escape no further through the reflections.

Weinberger swung round, tracking it. He grabbed in the air with both hands. The space above the actual waterbed was empty; the thing — Death — was not there. But in all of the mirror-cages all the reflections of his hands grabbed in unison. Weinberger seemed to know exactly what he was doing.

Death flapped frantically around the circuit, from one cage to the next, to escape those grasping hands. But it was all one and the same cage to Nathan.

He caught it.

In a cage thrice removed from the original the hands of one of his reflections closed on it and held it tight. His own real hands remained empty, as did those of all the other reflections of himself. But not that one reflected pair. Not those. They held the red thing high. The bat-moth. Death.

Death slashed at his hands with its wing-hooks, and gouged with its beak. Blood ran down the hands and wrists of that reflection. The real Nathan cried out in pain — and yet *his* hands showed no trace of wounds. Only the hands of that one mirror image which held the creature were being flayed and stabbed — yet Weinberger still felt the pain.

However much it hurt him, he refused to let go of the creature and continued to wrestle with it. It seemed quite uncrushable, if he was trying to crush it. With face distorted, he held on. His own two empty hands were cupped in mid-air, the sinews standing out. However much damage the creature did to his phantom hands, he still held it fast out there in the reflection. His finger bones had become a cage.

"He's over-reacting to the stimulant!" Sally called, seeing none of this. "What's happening?"

"He's fighting Death!" cried Jim. "He's caught Death and he's fighting it!"

"*What*?"

At that moment Weinberger faced towards where he knew Jim must be.

"Depolarise the glass!" he bellowed through the wall. "Transluce it!"

Jim tore himself away from the periscope hood, found the button and hit it.

Immediately he and Sally could both see through the cage. And of course, all the reflection worlds had disappeared. Weinberger was still wrestling — with thin air. His fingers still clutched — nothing. Jim could see what the man was doing, because he already knew what he was doing, but to Sally it must have seemed an insane mime.

Now Weinberger was tearing Death free so that he could hold it in one clenched hand — to throw it far away from him? No, now that he had succeeded he would never give up his hold on Death. He held that one imprisoning hand aloft in a salute. Baring his teeth, he grinned through his agony.

"Cut the current!" he ordered harshly.

Jim squeezed the bulb. The crackling hiss, which might have been the sound of Death's wingbeat or its wordless voice, faded away.

"Unlock the cage!"

Jim pulled the glass wall open, as ordered, then hesitated. Was he, in effect, letting Death — impossible, inconceivable, living Death — out into the world? Yet with the current no longer flowing, a mesh of frail wires hardly seemed any obstacle . . .

Weinberger saw his hesitation.

"You fool, I've got tight hold of it!" he shouted at Jim's face from the other side of the wires. He could easily burst through the wires by main force, but even in this extremity he had no desire to damage any part of his invention.

"It isn't *here*. Not in this 'here'! It's still in the reflection — that's where I've got hold of it!"

Had he? Had he really? Or was the pain so deeply etched into his punctured nerves and scoured fingers that he only thought he had? Was Weinberger only imagining that the struggle still went on in the way that an amputee feels phantom limb sensations?

Jim could not believe it. Weinberger continued to clutch the air — impeccably, and agonisedly. All the reflections had gone away to wherever reflections went when they were off duty. Yet, wherever that place might be, his reflected hands *must* still be mimicking, there, the shape and stance of his actual flesh and blood hands . . .

Jim tore the key from his neck, snapping the chain in his haste. He jabbed it at the lock twice before he succeeded in inserting it and turning it. At last he tugged the door open.

Weinberger crawled out and staggered erect before Jim and Sally, his clenched hand held at arm's length, triumph and torment written on his face.

ELEVEN

AS SOON AS Jim sank into the bean-bag seat, Resnick planted both hands firmly on the corner of his desk and began to pivot from side to side.

"This House is *not* a theatre of the absurd . . .!"

Resnick was upset, and if he sat down he might not be able to speak coherently.

Sally Costello had talked to Claudio Menotti, who had duly complained to the Master about her distress. Jim's cry — 'He's caught Death and he's fighting it' — had planted a dagger of disquiet in Sally's heart, which had been driven deep by Weinberger's frenzied emergence from the cage clutching an imaginary *something* at arm's length.

Resnick's scene-screen showed no sunset seascape this morning, but a smouldering volcano billowing smoke, on the verge of exploding.

'If he needs *that* to browbeat me,' thought Jim, 'then he can't quite manage it by himself.'

But Alice Huron was there too, sitting straight and tall, as well as Mary-Ann Sczepanski who seemed nervously intoxicated by the black, fire-flecked clouds. For the moment the etiquette of privacy and confidentiality had disappeared somewhere behind those plumes of smoke.

"What exactly *did* you mean when you said that, eh? And now that it's the morning after, how do you assess what happened?"

Jim considered.

Up in his room, Weinberger had not slept a wink all night. How could you get to sleep when your hand was being tortured? Jim doubted whether Weinberger could let go now, if he wanted to. His hand, and Death, were too intermixed: hooks trapped in bones, bones trapping wings. If, indeed, he was holding anything . . .

But Weinberger *knew* that he was holding something. His hand remained bent like an arthritis victim's, quite unable to flex. Yet to all outward appearances it was a perfectly unblemished hand. He did not sleep. He could not rest. He gritted his teeth, and held Death at arm's length.

"I believed I saw Death," said Jim defiantly. "It was like a bat. It was like a huge moth, though there was nothing flimsy about it! It had big crystal eyes. It was red — with a kind of redness, anyway. Maybe it was infrared."

"So now you can see in the infrared?" asked Alice Huron sarcastically. "Maybe that explains why those cameras saw nothing!"

This was true. When the videotapes were played back they had merely showed Weinberger jerking upright when he was injected, then scrabbling at the empty air for a minute or so — all on his own. Admittedly the record was confused by all the multiple images of Weinberger in the mirrors, but certainly no other creature was visible.

"It didn't register," agreed Jim. "Yes, it's exactly as though the tapes couldn't record light of the wavelength I saw. It's as though it came from a different spectrum entirely! But I swear that my eyes saw it."

"You *hallucinated*," said Resnick, still arcing about. "You hypnotised yourself by staring through that periscope into all those mirrors. Your attention drifted. You were almost in a state of sensory deprivation — and you know where those can lead! What was his name, eh? Mike Mullen, hmm? Your friend. According to your dossier —"

"Thank you for acquainting everybody with my dossier!"

"Necessary information, Jim! In case you don't realize it, we're in trouble. First the murder, now this. If this *fantasy* gets out . . .! But it won't, will it, Jim?"

"If you put Weinberger on public exhibition, it may."

"And we must do that — though I do take grave exception to the word 'exhibition'. Do you think you have us in a cleft stick, then?" Resnick danced from side to side as though to dislodge himself. "Let me remind you that in certain extreme circumstances a guide can be *required* to retire prematurely. If you follow me . . ."

"Oh, I do." Jim looked from Resnick's face to those of his accomplices of the stormy night at the chalet. His minions . . . Mary-Ann smiled automatically at the mention of retirement.

"All right, so Weinberger didn't find peace in his 'machine'," said Jim angrily. "But damn it, he's begun to purge his hostile feelings about death. That's what happened — don't you see? They're something he can seize hold of now. That's a darn good start."

"And what about your own hostile feelings about death?" asked Alice. "Since you're so positive that you saw the thing too!"

"Hostile —? What bloody nonsense! Just give me time with the man! Anyway, it isn't *your* job to decide."

Though *who* really did pull *whose* strings around this House?

"Maybe I developed a sort of quasi-telepathic linkage with Nathan," he admitted. "As a true guide should."

"With you in a state of sensory deprivation, that's understandable," said Resnick, in a more mellow tone. "You hallucinated, freely and grandiosely, when Weinberger sat up and began his phantom battle. You filled in the empty space in his hands. You gave it unreal life. So did Weinberger. He was torn out of deep trance by those stimulants. The blood was pounding through his heart valves, and probably through his eyeballs too. He saw that blood *personalised*."

'I couldn't have hypnotised myself,' thought Jim. 'I knew the risk. I looked away from time to time.'

"I do wonder," said Alice, "why Jim should have filled in the empty space with *that* in particular. That bat or fighting cock or whatever it was."

Or whatever: bat, rooster, moth — none of these, really. Or all of them. An alien composite, a creature not of Earth.

"Quasi-telepathy?" repeated Jim vaguely.

"It occurs to me," said Mary-Ann, "that we're all just *assuming* that you both saw the same thing." She sounded eager to help. "Okay, so it was a very powerful experience for you both, and you both saw something. But was it necessarily the *same* something? Was it the same experience? Have you asked Weinberger exactly what he saw?"

And Jim realized that he had not.

Because the event had been so very vivid, and because Nathan's clutchings had synchronised so perfectly with what he himself saw, he had indeed leapt to the conclusion that the thing that Weinberger saw himself fighting with, and the thing that Jim saw him fighting with, were one and the same.

Jim cursed himself silently, without letting any of the chagrin he felt show on his face.

He decided to lie. They *must* have seen the same thing. Otherwise, Jim's own private image of death — a secret even to himself, apparently! — was crazy and irresponsible. It was utterly childish.

Mary-Ann was not really being helpful, he decided. But she was eager enough: eager for him to fall into the trap of admitting his oversight, and so lay himself open to the charge of harbouring feelings which he was certain he did not possess, emotions which

68

were the opposite of what any true guide should feel. If he admitted the truth, he might as well resign here and now — if indeed the House allowed him simply to resign without at the same time demanding his premature retirement. As they could so demand. As they could.

"Of course I asked him," said Jim, hoping that no one else had asked Weinberger in the meantime. "We both saw the same thing."

"A case of powerful identification, then," said Resnick, reeling in the line just at the instant when the fish had been about to bite. "I agree that that's a fine thing in a guide — though in this case it does seem a *little* excessive. Okay, we're tolerant people here in Egremont. We always could afford to be, with Norman Harper at the heart of our society. *Could* afford to be, Jim. Past tense. Could."

"Weinberger experienced catharsis," said Jim, feeling more sure of his ground. "The hostile feelings have burst out of him, like an actual physical creature. As soon as he can *let go* of it, he'll be free of those feelings. Permanently."

"He only has to be free of them for the next few weeks," said Resnick. "I suggest that you go and hold his hand, till he opens it." The Master glanced at Alice Huron, who had leant forward as though about to say something. "We're in too deep to consider changing guides again. The bob-sled's half-way down the run." This sounded like a quotation from one of Norman Harper's poems.

Resnick bent to fiddle with a touch-pad behind his desk. The smoking volcano which had been looming over their discussion disappeared. In its place was a serene snow-clad mountain. All the inner fires and fumes and gobbets of lava were frozen by white Winter — the Winter of the world.

Jim left the office, aware that his own life was in a real sense beginning to depend upon Weinberger's good death.

Up in room 302 Nathan Weinberger lay slumped in bed, kept awake by pain. His clenched hand rested on a bolster to keep it from contact with the sheets.

How long could he succeed in holding Death at arm's length? When Death escaped from him at last, would it wing elsewhere

— or would it come straight to this room? Would it home in, and perch on the real hand whose mirror image at present held it at bay, captive in the realm of reflections? Jim wondered whether the pain allowed Weinberger much leeway for such speculations.

"My bones are coming apart," groaned Weinberger. "It feels as though they are! Maybe they aren't at all. This hand's still solid. Oh my too too solid flesh! But I can't *see* those other bones. I can only feel them. Oh hell, what I feel."

"Let go of it. Open your hand."

"I can't, Jim. I can't."

Jim leaned over Weinberger.

"We both did see the same thing, didn't we?" he whispered. "It was red, an unearthly red. It looked like a huge moth, or a bat — both at once. You did see that? That *is* what you're holding on to now?"

"Damn right it is!" Incongruously — confidingly — Weinberger winked. Or maybe the man's eye had developed a twitch. "Never fear, Jim — I shan't let you down."

"You'll let go," Jim promised. "You will."

"Ah, but will *you* let go?" Weinberger asked him roughly.

Jim had no answer to this but to shake his head.

"You believe me now, don't you?"

"I saw what I saw."

TWELVE

EVENING CAME, AND Weinberger had still not let go of the invisible thing in his hand. To Jim's surprise the sick man did not seem physically weaker. Rather, he seemed to be drawing strength from this prolonged bout of hand-wrestling with a hidden opponent.

Plainly the situation could not continue. Surely Weinberger must soon burn up all his reserves. If his life became endangered — prematurely endangered, Jim reminded himself, since Weinberger was dying anyway — would an emergency amputation of his right hand be in order?

It would be a castration, a cruel gelding of him.

If he lost his grip that way — like some thief in the old Middle East who had tried to steal a jewel from the Sultan of Death — it would be a cheat. Probably it would solve nothing.

Jim sat with Weinberger for an hour, his hand touching the other man's limp left hand, then he went away to visit the farmer with multiple sclerosis. The farmer was looking forward increasingly to an early retirement as the only sane alternative to the inevitable withering away of his faculties which the disease would bring. 'Don't sigh, die *high*,' was the motto in his case. It was a Norman Harper motto.

Jim returned to his own room at ten o'clock to catch some sleep, setting the alarm to rouse him at one in the morning.

Most people's bodily functions were at their lowest ebb around three o'clock in the morning. Three in the morning was the time when most deaths used to occur 'naturally' in the days before one could choose one's time. Around three o'clock, therefore — most probably tonight — Jim suspected that some kind of crisis might occur . . .

He let himself into Weinberger's room at one-thirty.

Weinberger lay awake, though his eyes were heavy and there seemed to be dark bruises under them. His hand was still clutched upon the bolster.

After ensuring privacy, as usual, Jim sat on the edge of the bed.

"I saw an old movie years and years ago," murmured Weinberger. "The movie was old, I was young. It wasn't your modern sort of movie. It had killing and torture in it."

"Didn't they all?"

"It took place in some desert, during some war or other . . .

> "It was all one war, with different faces,
> A carousel war, in different places,
> Turning, turning, burning, burning,
> Returning . . .

"Shit poet, you know, Norman Harper. Oh what have we come to? Anyway, the Arabs caught this man and tortured him. They tied him in a chair and ground his wrist bones back and forth with metal punishers."

"You remember that image especially?"

"Oh, it hasn't *suggested* anything, if that's what you think! No, I just feel like that fellow in the chair. Only, I don't have any secret to confess. So the pain can't stop. The torture just goes on and on.''

"There *is* a secret, Nathan. The secret is peace. Acceptance and unity. Fulfilment and completion.''

"When my hand's being screwed? Screw that!"

"It'll stop, as soon as you let it stop."

"Lame, Jim, lame. You saw Death too."

"But Death shouldn't hurt."

> "Don't complain, there is no pain
> When life's fulfilment you attain."

This time Jim couldn't tell whether Weinberger was quoting the murdered poet or parodying him.

They sat in silence for a long time, their fingers touching, watching the icebergs in the wall.

Occasionally Jim glanced covertly at his watch. He always wore the watch with its face on the underside of his wrist so as not to offend clients by checking the time ostentatiously. For the same reason he favoured an old-style watch with hands rather than an electronic one.

Two-fifteen.

Two-thirty . . .

Perhaps Weinberger would simply fall asleep at three o'clock. Outside, the House was hushed. It seemed hours since Jim had heard a sound of any sort. Not even the duet of their breathing was audible. Jim blinked, wishing that he had had the foresight to take a stimulant.

At a quarter to three Weinberger suddenly cried out like a woman in childbirth. His eyes goggled. Both his hands flexed, the fingers bending backward like an Asian dancing girl's. For just a moment Jim thought that the man had died, and his hand jerked towards the phone to call for a resuscitation unit.

But then Weinberger brought both hands together with a sharp clean smack.

"It's gone!" he cried. "It's damn well gone! Death's gone! Given up! Let go! Got away!" He pounded his hands together again and again.

And fell asleep, a moment later. Soundly asleep.

Jim checked the man's pulse and breathing. Both were fine. He reached for the phone again, to order the spy camera switched back on, but stopped himself in time. Nothing, but nothing, should disturb Weinberger while sleep healed his self-inflicted, phantom scars. Not a word, not a whisper. He would phone from his own rooms, instead.

He tiptoed out, locked the door silently and headed for the elevator.

It was with a huge feeling of relief and release that Jim climbed into bed.

Now that he was *persona grata* again, he wished he could share that sense of release, and his bed, with someone. But it was far too late, and besides, who was quite to be trusted? Maybe Marta Bettijohn was. Or perhaps he could apologize to Sally Costello. But no, she was under Menotti's wing, and operatic heroes could be jealous characters off-stage as well as on.

Before he fell asleep, he decided that it was time for that promised dinner excursion to the Three Spires restaurant down Egremont Mall, with Marta.

THIRTEEN

JIM WAS DREAMING of Marta. She was a Rubens woman, dressed in the skimpiest of lace streamers. These blew around her in the breeze, attached to little more than her nipples and the cleft of her sex — this was shaven and pink. Away from the chalet she skipped, in between the junipers; he pursued. The sky was monochrome, as were the trees and bushes. Yet Marta was rose-hued, and the sun was blood-red. Red, too, were the sails of yachts tacking on the lake. He gained on Marta. She beckoned him. They would act out the little death of orgasm on the shore.

But then the sails of the yachts became the wings of great moths. These moths beat into the air. They fluttered towards Marta and descended all about her. The moths sipped from her with long hollow tongues . . . Then Jim realized that far from sipping they were pumping something into her. Instead of deflating, Marta swelled like a balloon, becoming larger and larger and less and less substantial till she was quite transparent. Whereupon she floated off into the sky. Even though he had no wings, Jim flew after her to pierce the balloon, to pop it . . .

The trilling of the telephone woke him.

He clutched for his watch. It was late morning. He had forgotten to set his alarm, he had missed one appointment already and was late for the second one. Strange that no one had tried to rouse him till now.

When he picked up the phone Marta's voice spoke from the earpiece like an extension of his dream.

"Jim, I thought I should warn you. Your client Weinberger has been creating a fine old stir this morning —"

"He should be asleep! He should be sacked out for hours yet."

"On the contrary, he's remarkably energetic — I hear. Full of beans! Listen, Jim, he's claiming there's been a spontaneous remission of his illness. He says he's completely cured."

"*What?* Cured of his *cramp* — I know that! And just maybe he's cured of the mental complex that caused it. That *is* what you mean?"

"It isn't. Weinberger says that his cancer has all gone. Whoosh, just like that. He demanded a re-evaluation. Not a biopsy — he wouldn't let himself be cut open. A thermogram would suit him fine: a hot spot picture."

"Oh dear. Well, a thermogram will merely show that he's still riddled with cancer."

"Jim, I quite like you, so I should warn you —"

('As you liked me, last night?')

"— Noel got very annoyed, and had Weinberger rushed over to the Hospital with an escort, *tout de suite*. They already took the heat profile an hour ago. So far as they can tell, the cancer *has* all mostly gone. Or it's well on the way to going. They're still arguing about the exact interpretation of the thermogram results. But apparently Weinberger *is* cured. Rather suddenly."

Jim collected his scattered wits.

"A hysterical cure — is that it? Hysterical remission?"

"But Jim, he already officially retired. What's more, he's still a murderer! So he *has* to go through with his retirement. How likely is it now that he'll do it gracefully? The last time I saw Noel, he was lunging from side to side, shouting, 'What do we do now? Starve him to death? Drug the bastard with conditioners? Everybody would know!' The ball's in your court, Jim. And oh boy, is it

74

bouncing." She hushed her voice, so that he could hardly hear her. "It's as if he shot his own death into Norman — successfully. You know what that implies . . .

> "The other fellow dies
> In place of me.
> So here I'll pull the trigger;
> Here, I'll drop the bomb."

This was one of the poet's few ventures into free verse . . .
"I thought you should know."
"Fuck it," said Jim.
"What?"
"I said thanks a lot. For telling me, for waking me. I overslept."
Jim shook the hand set. "It's just like we're in bed together," he said to it from a distance.

He heard a click and a buzz as Marta rang off.

After dressing hastily, Jim hurried down to the room occupied by the woman with the heart condition. He apologized to her rather abjectly for having failed to keep their morning appointment. He went to other rooms, next, to reorganize his schedule for the day. That done, he descended to Noel Resnick's office. By now it was well after eleven o'clock.

"What's this I hear about Weinberger being cured?" he demanded accusingly as soon as he was inside the office. Accusation seemed to be the best policy. It was not Jim's fault that the man was cured. Nor was it Resnick's fault either, but Jim hoped that Resnick would overlook that detail, since it was he who had authorised the thermogram.

For once Resnick was alone. He was staring at a print of a human body in the form of a multicoloured mosaic.

Resnick promptly stood up, as though some invisible cord linked him to the door so that when this closed behind the visitor Resnick was jerked erect and his mouth tugged open to let his words flow easily.

'We're all puppets,' thought Jim: 'dolls in Death's puppet theatre. And Death is the director of the show — *according to Nathan.*'

75

On this occasion it seemed as if the Master would have to climb bodily on to his desk before he could get his tongue untied.

But Resnick triumphed.

"Been keeping your ear to the ground, eh Jim? Even while you were sound asleep . . . I guess that means you must have been sleeping on the floor!" He tapped the heat profile, like an acupuncturist jabbing needles. "Well, it's true. He certainly seems to be cured. The plot thickens!"

"What plot?" asked Jim.

Resnick ignored the question.

"It doesn't make a fart of difference to the final outcome of Weinberger's stay in this House," he went on. "But needless to say we can do without miracles of this sort. They breed a wholly false attitude to death. Eleventh hour reprieve, that kind of nonsense. If one word of this —"

Jim placed his own hands squarely on Resnick's desk, as though magically to paralyse the man — to control what he could say.

"Listen, Noel, let's cut a lot of corners right away. This 'cure' of Weinberger's has to be hysterical — at the same time as it's a physical fact. I'll take your word for it being a fact. So it's psychosomatic. Okay, that proves how deeply my therapy affected him. He's burnt out the cancer in himself with all that violent, hostile energy he was storing up. Now it's gone — like lightning rushing down a conductor to earth itself."

"Gone? Have you seen him this m-m-m-morning?"

Ah yes, the man *did* stutter. Jim pressed the desk harder, and pressed his point home.

"The next thing is, he'll adjust — because he *knows* that he killed a man. So there's no way out for him, is there? He'll come to terms and make his peace. But he couldn't do that as long as he believed that an actual hostile 'Death' was gnawing at his vitals. That's all changed now. There's only good death for Nathan now. He'll calm down." Jim was lying; he utterly doubted it. "If we play it that way, and I certainly shall, he'll see the natural logic. When he appears in public in a few weeks' time it'll be to . . . *commemorate* Norman Harper, who was in a sense his very own lightning conductor. No man could have done more for another man than Norman did, unwittingly, for him. But Weinberger should *never* have been allowed to get the way he did. It ought to have been spotted. I'm not criticising Mary-Ann, or this House —''

"B-b-but you are.''

Jim shook his head. "We all pull together. When we quit pulling, we retire to make way.''

"We sure do.''

"I shall see my client now to pick up the threads — I don't doubt that quite a few got severed during all the panic this morning. I don't want Weinberger interfered with again.''

Amazingly, Resnick nodded. He had swallowed this huge distortion — this shucking off of the blame on to him. Why? It must be because neither his 'operator' Alice, nor his minion Mary-Ann, was present. Resnick must really feel quite vulnerable. Even his tongue could betray him under stress. There was nothing more disconcerting than a giant of a man whose very words let him down.

And Resnick was definitely under stress. Jim had never wholly understood all the hidden strains and tensions which bound the various groups in society together: the Houses, the Peace Offices, the Census Bureau, the Re-Education Bureau — not forgetting such rich though numerically minor forces as the freezer freaks, or the disenfranchised religious groups which still clung on here and there. But he had his suspicions that society did not cohere as smoothly as it seemed to on the surface. He visualized society as a geodesic dome. A kick delivered to one part of it did no visible damage to that part. But the corresponding part one hundred and eighty degrees removed would be buckled. Norman Harper's murder — and now, Weinberger's spurious 'resurrection' — were two such almighty kicks, one overt, one as yet covert. The question was, if the kick was delivered here in well-adjusted, unblemished Egremont, what exactly would buckle, and where? Alternatively, what kicks was Resnick presently buckling under? If the Sino-Soviet War had been the huge kick from elsewhere on this globe which had propelled this land into the great Reappraisal of Death and the Restructuring, how national and even global might these events in Egremont turn out to be?

Weinberger had raved about 'beneficiaries of murder and accident' and about how the very best defence against Death would be a hydrogen bomb . . . Had Weinberger's imaginary creature, Death, gotten hungry for souls because too many souls had escaped it in a flash during the lightning Chinese-Russian war so many years ago? In that case Death must be like some sort of intelligent yeast or bacteria culture which was now trying to ensure its food supply by influencing men's minds . . . And Weinberger would be forced to feed himself to it. So must everyone who couldn't arrange a fatal accident for themselves, an accident about which they knew nothing in advance.

'That's sheer insanity,' thought Jim.

Removing his hands from Resnick's desk, he left quickly before Resnick could recover his poise.

"You haven't helped much," said Jim wryly to Weinberger.

Though Weinberger was still very gaunt, he looked remarkably perky.

"I can't believe you've had so little sleep."

"Oh, I never took much sleep in the old days. Even as a kid, I was a devil to my parents. I could manage on three hours a night. I'm no cat where sleep's concerned."

Jim noted this admission. The cycle of sleep and wakefulness was one of those balanced, complementary cycles (like day and night) which planted in the growing child the idea that there was a life beyond death; that death was not in fact the end. But if Weinberger had only ever taken brief holidays from wakefulness, how had these fantasies about 'Death' ever got planted in him? Ah . . . In Nathan's case the equation did not involve life and death at all. It consisted of peaceful death — versus violent death. Yes, that was it: violence versus peace. Weinberger's mind had known very little peace, because it was hardly ever switched off. So he couldn't stomach the idea of dying peacefully. Somehow he had to avoid a good death. But how? By forcing the House to surprise him into death? *That* mustn't happen . . .

At least Weinberger could not kill *himself* by surprise. That was one consolation, and indeed the watchful camera eye in his room was utterly irrelevant.

But more important than Weinberger's state of mind, more important than the lightning remission of his cancer, more important even than the political consequences, was . . . Death: the moth, the bat, which Jim now knew that he had seen. Jim's own dream had confirmed this in a way which he found curiously convincing. He had been keeping the thought of that creature under mental wraps ever since Marta's phone call.

Now he twitched those wraps aside, and immediately Weinberger seemed to sense that he had — as though the man had a nose for the pheromone of death, and Jim had just released a molecule of it.

"You'll help me catch it, won't you, Jim?"

Jim nodded.

"Do you suppose that two people can fit on to that waterbed of yours?" he asked, by way of answer.

"When?"

"Tonight."

"Who'll monitor us?"

"Not Sally Costello — the last time freaked her out. I don't really think we want witnesses now, do we? I can rig up something to switch the Faraday Cage on once we're inside. Your gizmo for powering up worked perfectly well on its own. We'll ignore the medi-sensors. As for the gilded key, that was a bit of indulgence on your part, wasn't it?"

"Who'll stimulate us? Who'll revive us when Death arrives?"

"I think we want to play this differently, the second time round. If we simply trap that thing, it's going to hurt us a hell of a lot. We must follow it instead. We have to find out where it comes from."

"But we'll be shut up in a glass box in *this* world — the ordinary world."

"When I was in Gracchus," said Jim, "my friend Mike Mullen — the one who died — was doing work on out-of-the-body experiences, as well as the death-trance."

"He was working on the astral plane?" Weinberger laughed. "That plane was grounded years ago. Unfit to fly. No wings."

"Well, Mike made it fly. Just towards the end, he said he flew — and he proved it to my satisfaction. Astral projection takes place in the ordinary world, though. It's like a sort of dream that let's you see what's happening miles away. Mike really wanted to 'fly' in the death-trance state too."

"To Heaven and back?"

"Whatever Heaven might be! Look at it this way. If there's a 'soul' that survives death —"

"Then it has to survive somewhere."

"Right. Mike recorded a hypno-tape for entering the out-of-the-body state. But he needed to get acquainted with the death-trance first — the oceanic unity state. First know your tides, before you raise the sails.''

"And he drowned."

"He drowned."

"The way *you* drowned."

"And no one revived him. I kept that hypno-tape of his. Because Mike and I were this close. Because that was all that survived of him, for me. If we use Mike's tape when we're heading in to death-trance, we stand a damn good chance of conducting an out-of-the-body journey *during that death-mimicry state*. While we're both playing possum. If only I'd been more interested in it at the time! But it was all oceanic unity for me — that's the sad thing. I guess I wanted to drown, not swim."

"Or fly."

"Like two flying fish! We'll do it too — we'll take off. I owe it to Mike."

"How about owing it to me?"

"Nathan, I'm giving you . . . my inheritance from Mike, an inheritance I didn't properly appreciate till now. I couldn't do more for anyone. I'm going to loot some conditioners from the pharmacy. We'll listen to that tape, as we sink deep down."

"Tonight?"

"Tonight."

So, instead of dinner with buxom Marta Bettijohn followed (perhaps) by equally delicious love-making, Jim was now committed — quite absurdly and unsexually — to go to bed with Nathan Weinberger!

He stood up.

"I intend to catch the Beadway along to your fine Mall now, Nathan. I'm going to lunch at your well-spoken-of Three Spires. And I shall drink a whole bottle of wine. All on my own."

It was a poor guide who spoke of the outside world to a dying man. But Weinberger was no longer dying — except in the official sense. And Weinberger would soon be going outside, with Jim — outside of the ordinary world, though the doors of the House still shut him in.

"Wine will make you sleepy."

"That's the general idea. I'll get my sleeping done this afternoon. Tonight — who knows? Maybe our bodies will get some rest while the soul goes hunting butterflies and chasing after bats, but I'm not counting on it.''

"Uh, shall we electrify the cage tonight?''

"Yes. Till we know more, I reckon we should vary our procedure as little as possible.''

Weinberger's right hand twitched.

"We don't want Death trapped in with us . . . Ah — but nor do we want it scooting off before we're ready to give chase! Yes, we'll electrify. We'll panic Death, then let it run for home. We'll need a time switch to cut the power automatically, once we've baited the beast.''

"Right. Though I can't say I relish the idea of hurting or scaring anything.''

"It was you who mentioned a hunt. A butterfly hunt.'' Weinberger stuck his index finger out like a pin and stabbed it into the palm of his right hand, skewering an imaginary captive.

"I'll be going now.''

"Run along,'' said Weinberger graciously. "*Bon appetit.*''

Jim failed to detect any hint of envy.

FOURTEEN

JIM HOVERED IN the doorway of 'The Montresor', looking for a waiter to show him to a table. Immediately his eye was caught by a streak of yellow against the mullioned windows overlooking the Mall: it was Ananda in his mustard robes. Ananda's companion was Marta Bettijohn.

Jim drew back momentarily, reviewing his decision to try the French restaurant in the Three Spires complex — a decision which he realized had been induced by Weinberger's parting remark. However, Marta waved him over with a cheery smile.

"You'll join us, of course?'' The invitation sounded perfectly genuine. Ananda, for his part, nodded tolerantly.

As Jim hesitated, Marta clapped her hands.

"Well, well, *well* — the lone gourmet! And here was me believing you were going to take the virginity of this place with *me*. And now you are going to, after all!''

With a rueful grin, Jim sat down. He felt somewhat trapped
— though happy enough in his captivity.

What, he wondered, was Ananda doing here? He had understood that the slight, swarthy, shaven-headed man was an ascetic
— a self-denier.

"Do you often eat here?" he asked him idly.

"Do you suppose it's out of keeping? Ah, Mr Todhunter, shall I
tell you my faith, my creed?" Ananda waited. It was not merely a
rhetorical question.

"Why not?" invited Jim.

"I believe in nothing — in absolute Nothing. So it doesn't
matter if I enjoy a rich meal — so long as I don't yearn for a repetition of the same. Which, indeed, could never be a satisfying
repetition. This will pass, as will I."

"You'll still enjoy the meal, though?"

"Let's hope so," said Marta brightly, looking up from the
engraved menu card.

"Denying the self does not involve punishing the self, Jim. That
is to give the self too much credit, too much importance."

"Sure."

"Nor do I score good karma points by self-denial. In what ledger
are they recorded? In none." Ananda leaned closer to Jim. "The
fact that I don't appear to resent your 'butting in' doesn't imply
that this was not a private *tête-à-tête*, just a little while ago. Where
better than a French venue for a *tête-à-tête*? But that situation has
vanished now. It has gone away. Another situation exists."
Ananda perched in his chair, looking like a chaperone.

Jim laughed nervously. "At least we're being honest."

"Because lies are stupid. Lies always pass away too, into the
truth."

For a moment this sounded to Jim like a veiled warning that his
planned intrigue of the coming night was already known to
Ananda. And to Marta. And to everyone . . .

As Jim watched Marta browsing nonchalantly through the
printed cuisine, he understood all at once that Ananda must sometimes go to bed with Marta — and that this implied no bonds, no
ties, no obligations of any sort, quite unlike the sticky web of Noel
Resnick's relationship with Alice Huron and Mary-Ann
Sczepanski. Ananda had actually detached himself from life, in the

82

midst of life. So Marta could never be hurt by him. Whereas Jim would . . . chase her; he would prick the balloon of her security and contentment, just as he had tried to do in the dream.

Jim visualized Alice Huron, in the chalet, bestriding Mary-Ann who in turn rode Resnick to climax. He imagined Alice using Mary-Ann as an inverted dildo, a sexual servomechanism with which to master the Master, while Alice herself enjoyed the slighter body of the woman. He saw Alice whipping Mary-Ann while she bestrode her, because Mary-Ann had failed to see through Weinberger to his rebellious heart, and so he had killed Alice's treasure. Yes, that was *true*, Jim decided; and he warmed to Ananda and Marta as a couple who co-existed without such sticky bonds.

"I guess I'll try the *Tournedos bouquetière*," announced Marta as the waiter arrived. She looked as though Ananda had said nothing out of the ordinary.

"*Moules à la provençale*," ordered Ananda, without consulting his menu.

"I'll try the *Tournedos* too," said Jim. To the wine waiter who hovered nearby, he added, "And a litre of *Rouge Maison*."

Marta glanced at him curiously, but asked nothing. Nor did she look set to say anything about her earlier telephone call, or the case of Weinberger. She and Ananda understood etiquette — they practised it perfectly in their own relationship.

Outside, sunshine flooded through the crystalline roof of the Mall upon saguaro cacti and branching tree euphorbias. A fountain danced, its plashing silenced by the windows.

Jim chewed a last artichoke heart, forked a piece of steak fat neatly to one side, and wondered what Weinberger would be eating off a tray, locked in his room. Eating? Just eating? He would probably be *devouring* now that he was cured. The imbalance between their eating circumstances did not bother Jim particularly. Both would pass, as Ananda would put it. Besides, Weinberger owed this meal to Jim. He refilled his glass.

"Have you much experience with the death-trance?" he asked Ananda.

"All the time, Jim. Every minute."

"No, I mean have you ever practised the death-trance state? What I really want to ask is: have you ever detached yourself

— your consciousness — from your body? Have you experienced . . . that kind of detachment?''

"Where would my consciousness go to? It is here, I am here. Here is everywhere — and nowhere.''

"Those are just words.''

"Which is precisely what is wrong with them. They establish a whole menagerie of 'somethings' all over the place, where really there are none. Even 'nothing' is a lying word — as is 'death' too. We have a word 'death', therefore it is 'something'. If we didn't have the word 'death' . . .''

"Then we'd all be out of a job," joked Marta, "and what's more, we wouldn't even notice it.''

"What are you really trying to ask me, Jim?''

Jim drank some wine. "Oh, I'm not.''

"Oh, you are.''

"Well, maybe, but . . .'' Did he want to ask Ananda to sit in tonight? And Marta too? No, he couldn't bear to think of it. Ananda and Marta were far across a gulf from him, and it was a far wider gulf than the one that separated those two from the tangled intercourse of Mary-Ann, Resnick and upright Alice Huron, whoreswoman with the invisible whip . . .

"No," said Jim.

"You must find your own way," said Ananda, "to the place which is no-place.''

This sounded so shockingly perceptive that Jim's hand jerked against his wine glass, upsetting it. A bloodstain spread across the tablecloth, soaking in. Ashamed, Jim hastily gathered his napkin over it.

"Let's get back," suggested Marta tactfully.

FIFTEEN

JIM SLEPT SOUNDLY till eight that evening and woke with a slight headache. He hunted in his valise for the hypno-tape which Mike Mullen had made back in Gracchus. Slipping the cassette into his pocket, he went down to the duty attendant's office.

Tonight the man on duty was Neilson. Or was the name Martinson? Jim couldn't remember. Somebodyson was reading a magazine which he hastily shuffled from sight as Jim came in.

Weinberger, in miniature on the only active monitor screen, lay abed reading a magazine too. Or at least he turned the pages now and then. Icebergs still floated in the wall vista. In the little screen they looked much closer together: about to shut their jaws on Weinberger. Had Somebodyson been reading the same magazine as Nathan? Maybe the attendant had been told to spy on Weinberger's every thought — but this was the only way he could work out how to do it.

"I'll be requiring privacy for most of tonight, starting around eleven. This might go on for a long time, so don't worry. I need a cassette player too —"

"Over there, sir."

"And a bridge-switch and some cable."

Somebodyson pointed.

While he was about it, Jim deftly removed the pass-key for the pharmacy.

He went to the pharmacy next and unlocked a drug cupboard, from which he filched a handful of conditioner pills out of a jar labelled *Neo-Harmaline-MDA*.

The popular name 'conditioner' was perhaps a little misleading. The untailored Harmaline alkaloid produced relaxation and withdrawal and vivid archetypal imagery; while MDA heightened insight and communication and reflectiveness, promoting too a sense of social concern — in this sense MDA was a 'truth drug', a drug which made one search for truth within oneself.

The chemically retailored package was somewhat milder in effect and side-effects than the source drugs: there would be no risk of vomiting or other upsets. Used therapeutically in the Houses, in the way that Jim had several times used it with disturbed clients, Neo-Harmaline-MDA produced a pleasurable feeling of detachment from life, an acceptance that this was the true course to follow, and a sense of the social importance of following it.

It should serve equally well to prepare Weinberger and himself for the suggestions of the hypno-tape without ruining their grasp on reality in any hallucinatory fashion. Too, it should help to protect them from any risk of actually dying when they reached the 'thanatos' rhythm stage, because it would condition them to accept the taped commands to shunt themselves from the oceanic

85

'thanatos' state into the out-of-the-body state. There would be sufficient thanatos to turn on the pheromone tap and lure Death; but not enough for Death to be able to carry them off. Instead, they would hunt Death together through its own domain.

If, thought Jim, Mike Mullen's tape worked as promised . . .

But it would. Oh it would. Mike had been a man of superb insight.

Jim offered up a silent prayer of thanks to Mike's dead soul, dissolved (so he hoped) in the ocean of unity — since he had nothing else to pray to. And a muted vow of vengeance too, since if Nathan was right then Mike Mullen, playing possum, had become one more victim of the Death parasite. But a moment later Jim withdrew his vow. '*That*,' he thought, 'remains to be seen. And thanks to Mike (bless him) we two shall see it tonight.'

As though warding off evil, Jim made the sign of the rosette: the circle of life, completed; the flower, gathered.

Gathered — by what?

On the pretext of collecting a time-switch, Jim returned to the monitor room and replaced the pharmacy key without Somebody-son realizing that it had ever been removed. Then he took the elevator down to the blue room in the basement to rejig Weinberger's cage for full operation from inside.

By now his mild hangover had disappeared.

Jim collected Weinberger at quarter to eleven, and together the two men went down to the blue room.

They both stripped to vest and shorts for comfort, Weinberger draping his yellow robe over one of the two chairs, Jim folding his sandy suit, shirt and unravelled bow tie over the other.

Weinberger, who was to wear the thanatos skullcap, preceded Jim into the cage and rolled across the rubbery waves to the far side. Jim hunched his way inside on hands and knees. Turning, he pulled the door of the Faraday Cage till it was almost shut. With the cord he had connected earlier, he tugged the glass wall till it clicked into position — it was already opaque from the outside, a mirror from the inside, as were the other walls and roof panel. Then he closed the wire door tight.

Jim fed low power to the cage, then fed himself one of the heart-shaped orange pills. Weinberger accepted a pill, though he had trouble summoning up enough saliva to swallow it. He chomped his jaws as noisily as a wine taster before, with a wriggle of his Adam's apple, the pill slipped down his craw.

Now the hypno-tape was playing. Mike Mullen's lilting, lost-forever voice instructed them like a lullaby composed not to send the listener to sleep but to transport him to another mode of consciousness. Persuading, evoking . . .

Jim felt himself drift out among the multiple images of himself in phantom-land. He was all of those Jim-reflections; they were all him. He raised a hand in salute; each of them raised a hand. But whose will and whose intention raised that hand? 'The third Jim to the right,' he thought whimsically. If they were all identities, did they think thoughts too? In which case, what did they think about him lying here — in the prime dimension?

What was a 'person', anyway? A person was a cluster of different minds — different mental systems — each with its own unique spectrum. A person was a constellation, and his physical body was a cluster of different organs in symbiosis, and all the cells in those organs were descended from a primitive symbiosis long ago — from the mutually advantageous union of organisms which were originally independent. Just as the body died constantly throughout life, its cells replacing themselves, so did the mind die too, replacing its mental systems with new ones. A person's mind seemed to be continuous in time but it wasn't really continuous at all. On the contrary, it was quite often discontinuous. Why shouldn't he achieve a new sort of discontinuity right now? Why shouldn't he invest his awareness, his point of view, in Domain B, or C, or D instead of here in the prime domain? For a moment he had no idea which domain 'he' was really in. Inevitably he, as observer, would *seem* to be at the centre of all the other domains — wherever he 'really' was . . .

So many other 'Jims', curving away from 'himself' in the mirrors!

Multiple Weinbergers curved away too, and he felt a growing sense of fusion with the other man: an interleaving of their bodies, lives and minds.

Shifting his head, he stared up at the reflection of himself above. The single reflection, since the bed he lay upon was not a mirror. Or did he stare *down* at himself, from above? He no longer knew which. He stared into his own eyes, which returned his stare. He understood that his astral body was already waiting up above, just as Mike Mullen promised that it would be. His eyes began to close. It seemed to him that the eyes of his other self stayed open, still watching him.

'I'm dying,' he thought; or did the tape tell him this? 'Descending. Sinking through myself. Rising into that other self, too . . .'

"*Detach yourself . . . Flow in, flow out . . .*"

The blue basement room no longer existed. The world had gone away. All of his life was coming to a climax here — and the life of another person too, knotted with his. Surely this was the very first time in the history of the world (but where had the world gone?) that two people had shared the very same death instead of dying separate deaths . . .

"*Like breath departing . . . ebbing . . . the breathing out of the whole world . . .*"

Reflections. And their cousins, shadows . . .

The spirits of the dead used to be known as 'shades' — because they were shadows cast by the living person upon some hidden screen: shadows which continued to exist and move about even when the living person had died . . .

A reflection must be an intermediate state between the living and the dead, between the substance and the shade . . .

He began to sense a zone of shadows beyond the world of walls and rooms and buildings, beyond the world of living bodies, grass and trees. But that shadow zone was light, not dark.

Perhaps, through his mind's eye, he saw that zone in photographic negative. For it seemed to him that the real world had grown very dark while that other world grew bright.

Rapture glowed in him. It was the same rapture that he had known when he drowned, and which he had recaptured once in Gracchus . . .

Ah, he was drowning on this water bed . . . Quite suddenly the three episodes of rapture linked up with each other. They were one and the same, and it was the only real moment in his life. They — or it — encircled his life in a stream. And into that stream he swam.

Rapture: it was as intense as an orgasm, so that his whole self drained into that rapture. But it wasn't localised in any one part of him . . .

He smelt a salty sweetness like spilt semen. The smell was in his mind. He was smelling the pheromone of death . . .

"*Now. Do not die. But shunt. Leave your body alive behind you. Leave it waiting for you. It will be linked to your spirit by a silver cord. That cord can stretch for a million miles and never snap. Ease your feet out of your flesh-feet, as you would ease them out of shoes. Ease your hands out of your flesh-hands, as out of gloves. Unpeel the jacket of your arms, roll down the trousers of your legs. Strip the vest of your chest. Free the butterfly from the chrysalis — let it take wing!*"

Jim opened his eyes.

He understood that Weinberger had also opened his eyes at the same moment.

Together, they gazed down upon themselves — and the selves on which they looked down did not return their gaze. How still and mute those two corpse-selves lay below, with eyes closed.

To right and left he could see no reflections of their bodies, but only empty boxes defined by faint, waxen, gilded membranes which presently melted into a golden fog. The two men were afloat in a honeycomb with a black floor. And the cell walls of this honeycomb? Those were the electrical forces of the Faraday cage, reflected and reflected: a network of energy.

In the next moment the red creature, Death, perched upon Jim's chest below. And the golden walls intensified like sunrise. He heard the bee-hum of the increased power.

Death vanished momentarily. It reappeared upon Weinberger's chest and made a foray towards his neck, then leapt back. It seemed confused, disorientated, as it would be by finding the same death doubled — shared and synchronised — and this not even being a genuine death. No wonder it was perplexed. Appearing and disappearing, it shuttled from one man to the other. But it was more in existence than out of it. It was probably present all the time now. Its flickerings and shiftings were quantum jumps from one location to the next with no real interval of nonexistence in between.

'Where have all our own reflections gone to?' wondered Jim. 'We're a sort of reflection now, ourselves — and a reflection can't see another reflection. It only sees the substance — the original. But we can still see all the cages. So Death's still trapped. By us, and by the electricity.'

Death did not look so frighteningly rapine tonight. There was an eerie, unearthly beauty about the creature. Though surely a cruel beauty.

"Whatever *is* it?" Jim whispered. He spoke without stopping to wonder what medium would carry his voice. But he heard his own words clearly. As did Weinberger, who gestured impatiently.

"We're up and out, Jim. We made it!" he crowed.

Weinberger seemed less concerned with the nature of the creature than with the bliss of hanging above it like a hawk about to drop on to another bird which had got grounded, tangled in a wire trap. He spread his scrawny arms as though soaring in the thermal above his own body heat. His out-thrown hand buffeted Jim's floating body, but softly. If it had been moving more swiftly his hand might have passed right through Jim, their substances mixing like amoebas in reverse.

By partly shutting his eyes, Jim thought that he could make out a silvery thread tethering Weinberger, kitelike, to his possum body. A similar thin thread seemed to link Jim to the 'dead' original below.

Just then a sudden change came over their surroundings. The time switch must have cut the power to the cage.

No longer were they adrift in a honeycomb of translucent golden wax. There was fogginess, still, but it was a white fog which filtered light from beyond it — 'beyond' being on all sides, though perhaps more so in one direction than another. It wasn't really a fog at all, decided Jim. It was simply an out-of-focus quality as though he was a short-sighted man who had suddenly lost his spectacles. By moving closer, in whichever direction, he ought to be able to see the nature of that foggy light more clearly . . .

At the same time he was aware of shadows too: a whole pyramid of shadows. The House of Death loomed over them in the ordinary world. Beyond its shadowy bounds was Egremont. Beyond Egremont was the rest of the shadowy planet.

Jim realized that he could choose to fly into those shadows of reality, or else he could fly into the white fog. Both were present. Both were separate and distinct.

If they chose to fly off into the shadows they could range throughout the ordinary world, visiting Lake Tulane or Gracchus or anywhere else they desired. They could pass through shadow walls into locked rooms. They could spy on ardent lovers. They could let themselves be drawn to old haunts, to old friends. They could be voyeurs, spectators — unseen and unfelt by the living who were inhabiting their ordinary bodies. The silver threads would be their lifelines, however far they ranged.

It was very familiar, that shadow world. With its power of familiarity it drew them. Because they were alive.

But if they flew into the fog, towards the source of light rather than towards familiar shadows . . . *where to, then*?

It was so much easier to concentrate on the shadows of the things they knew! The shadows drew, the fog was out of focus.

Red Death hopped from body to body, below. With its sharp little beak or the scalpel hooks on its faery wings it might cut their silver threads of life! If it could find those threads. If that was what it was hunting for . . .

It had quit hunting now. It had stopped its questing from one body to the other.

As though aware that it was no longer caged it flew up suddenly, flickeringly, towards them. Weinberger grabbed for it. It darted to one side, avoiding him. Its crystal eyes glittered at the two floating reflection-bodies: registering them, discarding them from its attention. It flew off into the fog. Not into the shadow.

As it winged fog-wards it seemed to stabilize. No longer did it flicker. Out 'there' it was more real and permanent. Yet it flew with a curiously veering style of flight, arcing this way then the other way as though incapable of flying in a straight line.

Weinberger thrashed his empty hand about in annoyance. It was with his left hand that he had tried to snatch and bait the creature. Perhaps the nerves in his right hand still remembered all too painfully what had happened last time.

"Give chase, Nathan! We mustn't lose sight of it!"

Already the creature was passing out of focus. Already it had become less of a definable 'something' and more of a reddish anything swinging from side to side like a pendulum bob which got smaller with each swing.

The two men moved as one into the fog, without thinking how they moved, merely willing it. They clove the fog as sleekly as two seals.

SIXTEEN

VERY SOON THEY found that they could no more fly a straight course than the creature did. What seemed to be fog was actually an enormous clutter of prisms and polyhedra of many different shapes and hues, afloat in all directions. These 'fog crystals' were all approximately the same size: just a little smaller than the cage for Death itself. They were great jewels, drifting, jostling and rotating within the ether of their flight.

If they had flown in a straight line they would soon have struck one of these — and perhaps plunged inside it, for there was something about the faces of the crystals that suggested still pools rather than hard sheets of glass. Most of the crystals seemed to repel them gently, as they passed among them. But a few attracted them, pulling softly . . .

Now that they were in the midst of the crystal horde the fog was no longer white at all, except away in the distance. (Or were they in the midst? Maybe they were still only on the very fringe.) The immediate vicinity was multicoloured with the spillage from all the floating prisms and gems. Further off, where all the colours of the crystals recombined, was that hint of white light. Here, though, was ruby. Nearby was sapphire. Above, was garnet. Beyond was emerald . . .

"Wait!"

Intrigued, Jim slowed and hovered by a ruby larger than himself which was turning very slowly, weightlessly. He pressed closer to it; it seemed softly to resist him. A safe one, this ruby, somehow . . . It did not want him to dive into it. (But how could it 'want' anything?)

Weinberger hung beside him impatiently, though reluctant to press on alone. Anyway, they had almost overhauled Death. They could allow it a little leeway.

92

As Jim shifted about, trying to see something inside the ruby, suddenly the jewel space opened for him — though he knew that he was still safely outside it. Its interior faces unfolded like falling cards; and he saw, as through a fish-eye lens, a world: a world in miniature, yet whole, full-grown.

It was a world of crystal crags and shattered blocks and lakes of solidified lava. Bubbles had burst in the lava before it had cooled and set into great eggcup shapes. An angry, gritty wind blew through that world. A large red sun hung in the sky, providing the ruby light. People nested in the lava eggcups which sheltered them somewhat from the grit and wind and which concentrated a little the feeble warmth provided by the sun. It did not look like a happy or a comforting world . . .

"Do you see? Don't look too long! *Do you see*?"

Somehow, Jim feared that if he looked too long into the jewel, despite its soft, almost 'satisfied' repulsion of him he might end up inside it.

"No . . . what? *Yeah* —!"

"Come on, then."

They chased Death again, recovering their lost ground, and paused again beside a smoky garnet. Catching the angle of vision for this jewel, they saw two amber suns inside. The suns were oval, linked by a curving golden whip wrapped round their waists. The world which they illuminated was a jungle hell of swamp and tangled islands riotous with violent vegetation. Great pink and white pitcher plants yawned wide their gullets like rows of hungry blotched carp standing on their tails. Sundew-bushes spread wide diadems of sparkling sticky liquid light. Vines thrashed about and slithered like snakes, trying to strangle each other with knotted nooses. Hummingbirds with dagger beaks hovered in the sanctuaries (for them) of anemone-shrubs whose polyp tentacles suckered other little bodies, and skeletons, to them. These bright birds shot forth like darts from their deathly havens to stab lurid butterflies. Venus's fly-traps held spikes agape.

A naked woman stood on the only bare spit of land; a writhing tentacle-arm sprouted from her chest like a hugely elongated third breast. She advanced across the spit towards an island, waving her breast tentacle before her, and as she waved it the sticky blobs of sundew withdrew from her path, and the pitcher plants shut their gullets so that she could stride across them like stepping stones, and the spikes of the fly-traps snapped shut prematurely. Somehow her tentacle controlled the vegetation. The woman howled at the sky, and began to sing . . .

"Alien worlds: is that where dead souls go to?"

"I doubt it, Jim. Alien worlds fill up with alien souls, not human souls."

"Is that woman human?"

"I guess she's as human as she can manage to be."

The jungle thrashed about while the woman sang. She was playing it, compelling it to bend this way and that, forcing the plants to open up again and eat each other: swallow each other, strangle each other, tear each other to pieces, dissolve each other — till there was a knoll of land completely cleared in the middle of the island for her to lie down on to sleep.

"If that's how she gets her rest, I'd hate to see what she does when she's feeling lively!"

The woman was raw power.

"That's *her* world," said Jim. "It's the world she fantasizes, made real. It's full of all her lunacies come true. You're right: it isn't an alien planet at all. It's an imagination world. Hers."

"Or ours. We could be imagining her."

"I don't think so. But if we dived into a crystal we could check that out."

"No thanks. Death hasn't dived into any of them yet."

They sped on.

Inside a third jewel, a yellow zircon, was a velvety garden with yew hedges, arbours, bowers, pergolas, gazebos. The garden stretched on and on over hill, down dale. Obscene black statues stood about the lawns and peeked from behind bushes. A naked orgy was in progress on one of the lawns. All the participants had grossly distorted sexual organs, or else their sexual organs were in the wrong place. One man sported a great penis for a nose. Another man's whole head was a penis with eyes and nose and mouth. Worse yet was a mobile penis on legs which seemed to have been torn out of a giant's groin and set down to run about. One woman's face had labia where her lips should have been and nipples instead of eyes; her actual eyes were set in her breasts . . .

They watched this world for more moments than they had

94

intended, forcing themselves to stay in place despite the soft contrary thrust. The infrared creature had winged so far ahead of them by the time they let themselves drift away that it had almost disappeared.

Hastily they sped above, beneath and around many other world-crystals. More seemed to attract than to repel them now. Jim couldn't be sure, having no wish to yield to their attraction, but it seemed to him that those crystals which did attract were like blanks with no world inside them, 'wanting' someone to enter and stamp their own vision upon uncreated territory.

Away to one side something tiny — not Death — caught Jim's notice.

"Look!"

It was a little wriggling brown thing . . . he couldn't make it out. Then Red Death was there too. Death dodged out from around a shoal of crystals. But it was a different Death from the one that they were chasing. That one still raced on ahead. This second Death dived at the wriggling thing, then veered away — just as the wriggling thing struck a golden crystal. Instantly the crystal convulsed, and split. It became two golden crystals that slowly moved apart. One of these crystals remained 'blank', but the other was full of a play of light and transformation for a short while before it settled down.

The second Death flew off at speed. It had been like an old warplane releasing a bomb or missile: namely, the wriggling thing.

Weinberger called out something about Tibetans.

"What Tibetans? They're all dead, in the War. Russian bombs, Chinese bombs, radiation . . ."

"The old Tibetans! They said that if a dead soul follows the wrong light after death, then it winds up in some foul alien world. That's what these crystals are — and we've seen how foul they are inside. There must be billions of them — enough for everyone on Earth, past, present, future! One each."

"One each? But I saw more than one person in that first one. And what about in the orgy world? I don't know if those were all people, but . . ."

"Did you see more than one *real* person? Or were the others all just fantasy actors and actresses — the furniture of one dead soul?"

Jim shuddered. It was far better that the soul should *not* survive death, if the alternative was this: to be deluded for ever more!

Deluded. Or, perhaps, *creative*? Creating a whole world for oneself? A world of one's own choice?

"Somewhere in all this there must be paradises."

"Must there? Oh, there once may have been — and in that case I guess there still will be. But who believes in a heaven now? And if you don't believe, you've crapped out. Besides, who's to say that any of this exists for man's benefit? Who's to say, Jim?"

"Maybe the dead souls in those worlds could say?"

"Jim, I see Death as hauling souls out, and dumping each one into a separate crystal — to *fertilise* it. So that Death can feed on it. So that Death can have fun. Hell, we just saw that other Death do that! It dumped a soul."

"If that wriggling thing was a soul . . . That Death was like a warplane, firing a missile."

('Is that exactly what I saw? Was that exactly how it happened?')

"Death's a parasite, but it's an almighty powerful one. We're like the aphids that it milks. Here is its honeycomb, and we're its honey. Our fantasies are. Our anguish is. All our hallucinations, made real. It squeezes our lives into those crystals," Weinberger said.

"If it catches us. But what about all those sudden, accidental deaths which happen too quickly for Death to get there in time? The ones that give off no signal? Where do those souls go, damn it?"

"Maybe they reach the white light beyond, whatever it is. Peace, union . . . I see Death as —"

"I don't see Death at all. *Anywhere*. Where's it gone to, Nathan? We've lost it."

They sped faster, hunting, trying to pick up the trail. They failed. After a while they drifted to a halt.

Without the infra-red creature to follow they were lost in this shifting three-dimensional maze. They had no way of telling where Death's roost lay, or in which direction the exit from the maze existed, if indeed there was any exit. The white light might be in any direction, or in all directions. Around them the jostling of the crystal domains seemed to go on forever. Now that they had lost their impetus the two men concentrated on avoiding those crystals which pressed slowly towards them. And they concentrated on not getting separated from each other.

"Up there!" cried Weinberger, pointing.

Another red blur came arcing this way and that towards them.

It was yet another Death. And this Death held something struggling in its beak. A worm? No, it was one of those wriggling brown things — and now Jim had no doubt what it was.

It was a human soul: a wormlike miniature of a person. It had a human face, and it wriggled. It was like something that had crawled out of the top of the spinal column. It was like a sperm, writhing its way through the maze . . . until it met the great egg of a crystal and bored its way inside. But this soul wasn't free to swim. Death was bearing it along to the destination chosen for it. How that soul struggled! How impotently, how ineffectively! If it fought free of Death's beak it could perhaps swim right through the maze, to bliss and unity. But Death held it tight.

> 'Our soul's like a worm,
> And a bit like a sperm,'

thought Jim, in a Norman Harper way.

There came a brief flurry of red creatures, darting and dipping through the crystals like a flock of swallows. Each carried a single worm in its beak.

One of these Deaths veered close to the two men, and for a moment Jim clearly saw the face of the worm it had captured. It was that of an elderly woman. Her little eyes bulged in horror and surprise.

Those Deaths flashed by with their prey, which they would thrust into some crystal to ferment it into an intoxicating, toxic world which they would sip on like wine, growing drunk on the soul's deranged dreams.

The two men chased after the flock of Deaths. But the Deaths were all flying by slightly different routes. As Jim and Weinberger tried to chase them all at once, and still remain together, they collided. Their reflection bodies tangled.

The mixing felt like a breathing in of warm smoke by their arms and legs and torsos. There was a stickiness to it, as if the smoke was suffused with honey.

Before they could fully pull apart, a diamond crystal swung in

97

their way. It drew them to it at the same time as it slowly bore down on them. If they had not been pulling at cross purposes they could still have steered clear . . .

They hit it. They broke through its face, like two divers through a pool. Then they were inside the jewel.

At once the whole crystal fog vanished . . .

SEVENTEEN

IN ITS PLACE, was a world . . .

And the world was a place of blue mossy glades with clumps of feathery white trees stuck in the ground around the glades like so many goose-quill pens. The landscape was all blue and white. The ocean and icebergs of Weinberger's scene-screen had been transformed into moss and trees — the same colours, but different forms.

A sun was about to rise. Already, the spillover of light gave the cool dawn air a pearly hue. Some stars were still visible in the sky. Their winking lights were faintly ruby and topaz and sapphire. Those stars must be the other crystals, by now infinitely far off.

This world seemed curiously empty. It was incomplete — merely sketched in. Even the trees looked as though they had just been poked into the surface. But at least it held no obvious threats — unless it threatened to starve them of food, or variety; it was simply quiescent.

"Compared with those others it's fairly pretty," said Jim as they stood looking around. "But there isn't a lot to it, is there?"

"That's because we didn't put enough into it! We couldn't, because we're still alive. Or maybe we cancelled out each other's wishes? If it's normally a case of one dream-world per soul, well, with two of us involved either you'd end up with bizarre paradoxes, or you'd get something like this — a sort of minimal limbo. At any rate, there isn't very much for Death to get itself excited about here!"

The sun rose suddenly, flooding the world with white light. That sun was far away and considerably smaller than the Sun seen from Earth, more the apparent size of Venus. But it was incomparably brighter. After the first blinding glance, which left afterimages dancing like ball lightning among the trees, it was impossible to look even briefly in its direction.

Jim and Weinberger set out hastily for the closest shade. Their ability to fly had vanished.

As soon as they took their first steps across the blue moss, however, the whole surface began to ripple. With each footfall it rose and fell like a waterbed. The ground was merely a coating over liquid — as though it had not yet had time to set firmly.

Weinberger's foot broke through the moss. He stumbled, recovered himself then bounded on in great ground-hugging strides which somehow kept him ahead of the holes which his feet punched in the surface. Arriving at a feather-tree he clung to it.

Jim reached another nearby tree and clutched it. The two men stared at each other across a strait of the deceptive moss.

"Whoever dreamed this up?" shouted Jim. "How do we *go* anywhere?"

"Run, and hope for it?"

"There could be *things* under the moss. Hungry things."

Together, they had created this world. (Or, as Weinberger suggested, cancelled out each other's dream.) But to the extent that this world must partly be Jim's own creation, it occurred to him that it was all very well illuminated and enlightened up above, yet was actually hollow and deceitful, with no real solidity, but only treacherous amorphous depths. In the same way as his own world of good death and oceanic peace was hollow — and had always been so?

He rejected the idea. This world was frail because he wasn't truly dead; nor was Weinberger. That was all.

"We could try rolling," suggested Weinberger. "We'd spread our weight that way."

"Rolling about like self-propelled logs? But where to?"

Maybe the water under the skin of this world was indeed the ocean of unity and peace? If so, Jim couldn't see it for what it actually was because of all the blue moss . . .

"We have to find somewhere more substantial, Jim!"

And if they did? If, by searching for firmness, somehow they enforced firmness on this world?

"Then we'd be really trapped! Don't you see? This is no place for us. We've got to get *out* of here — right out."

"Just show me how, and I'll be right behind you. Meanwhile, how about rolling over to this tree?"

"No, you come over here."

"Chicken."

Both men laughed. Then they laughed again, rejoicing briefly in their ability to laugh.

As the tiny, white-hot sun climbed higher, sweaty heat came in the wake of the intense light. The feather-trees began to furl their foliage around their thin trunks. Before long the two men were sheltering behind mere spikes of a girth hardly greater than one of Weinberger's scrawny legs.

And Jim thought: if they were to die here, of heat-stroke and thirst and exhaustion; if the silver threads which bound them to Egremont were to snap — would this world suddenly take on a more solid face? Would the waters recede — or evaporate — to reveal hard lands beneath?

That silver cord! Of course.

He tried to twitch it so that he could reel himself back to the waterbed in Egremont. He felt a slight lessening of his weight, but nothing else happened.

As the sun burned ever more fiercely, the moss turned brown, at first in isolated patches, then everywhere. As it shrivelled, it broke up to reveal pools, then open rivers of blue water.

The moss must simply be a growth of the night — a twelve hours' wonder of fecundity which repeated its life cycle every night between dusk and dawn. Now it had spored or done whatever else it did. Crisped by the sun, it decayed.

Slowly the spikes of the trees began to tilt and bob and float free. Most still balanced precariously on their underwater root-mats, but others keeled right over. Maybe the 'trees' were nothing more than hairy stalks or filaments of the blue water-moss. Maybe there was only one kind of plant life here after all . . .

Like sailors lashed to masts, the two men clung to their frail sanctuaries. Inevitably, and quite soon, their weight bore the furled trees over, dipping lower and lower.

Jim felt resigned. This was the ocean, after all. And they were going to drown in it. He was going to drown again.

Weinberger whimpered. He had never drowned before.

Both men were sinking into the water: thigh deep, waist deep . . .

'Peace,' thought Jim. Relaxing his grip upon the tree, he raised both arms above his head and let himself go under.

And felt himself wrenched back violently by the scruff of the neck, like a rubber ball on elastic . . .

EIGHTEEN

NOEL RESNICK, Alice Huron, Ananda and Somebodyson clustered around the open cage door, staring in at the waterbed. The glass walls were transparent. The entry side was hinged wide open. Sally Costello moved away, clutching an empty hypodermic syringe.

"Good morning to you both," said Resnick tartly.

"I hope you had sweet dreams?" enquired Alice. Her chin jutted as she peered through the wire mesh above the door, not deigning to stoop. She looked down her nose at the two men as though inspecting them through an old-fashioned lorgnette.

Jim sat up.

"Dreams? No, not *dreams* . . ."

Beside him, Weinberger sat up too.

"Visions, perhaps? And you, Client Weinberger, I trust that you feel closer to the noble art of dying?"

Ananda laid a restraining hand on Alice's arm, while Resnick shuffled about, looking embarrassed.

Weinberger blinked at Alice and the Master; then he simply laughed.

Alice nodded to Ananda, acknowledging the growing pressure of his hand. She stepped back, impatiently clunking the rings on her fingers together.

Resnick gestured at the clothes draped over the two chairs.

"Would you two care to get dressed?" To Somebodyson he said, "When Client Weinberger is ready, kindly escort him to his room."

"What time is it, Noel?" Jim asked. He had left his watch in his jacket pocket.

"Going on for eleven. That's eleven a.m., in case you've completely lost track of time."

"Damn it, that means I've missed . . ."

"Correct. Not that a couple of missed appointments are —"

"— a matter of life and death?" put in Weinberger, acidly.

"Even though I seem to recall that it was you, Jim, who was going to concentrate on everyone alike!"

"You promised not to interfere," said Jim. "You gave me your word."

"Did I? Yes, I suppose . . ." Resnick looked unhappy.

"The point is," butted in Alice, "you've been in here for about twelve hours. And it looked as though you were going to stay here almost for ever — till you wasted away." She cast a derisive glance at Weinberger in his vest and shorts.

"So don't blame Sorensen," said Resnick quickly. "He's half-way through his second shift by now. He gave you a lot of time."

Sorensen yawned dutifully.

"But it isn't up to a duty attendant to decide —"

"Be reasonable, Jim. As Alice says, you were going to stay here for ever."

"Like Sleeping Beauties," said Sally Costello sweetly.

"Bewitched, entranced. Right." Resnick smiled gratefully.

The two men scrambled out of the cage and began to pull on their clothes. Promptly Alice Huron sat down on one of the vacated chairs. 'Sitting in judgement,' thought Jim. Resnick gripped the back of the other chair and pivoted about that fulcrum from side to side, like a nervous lion tamer.

Any notion of privacy had obviously disappeared, so far as Alice Huron was concerned. Now that Weinberger had been led away, she questioned Jim relentlessly, while Resnick bobbed about, allowing it.

"A dangerously interesting set of fantasies," she said at last. "Just what the hell did you expect, taking Neo-H with that nut?"

"Truth," replied Jim coldly. "The truth."

"And do you really think you found the truth? Did you discover the secret master plan of Death, about which nobody else knows one blue damn?"

"You found that place because you looked for it," said Ananda gently. "But it was indeed no-place, an illusion of your mind. You were both *alive*, Jim. Had you been dead, there would have been no such illusion. A philosopher once said, 'Death is not an experience in life; death is not lived through.' Nor did you live through death,

102

my friend. Nor did you come back to life. You were alive all the time. So how could you know anything about death?''

Jim shrugged.

"*Nothing* is known about death, because death is nothing,'' went on Ananda. "It is no-knowledge. Which is why there is nothing to fear, or to know.''

"You were *conditioned* by Weinberger,'' said Alice firmly.

"That's all too likely,'' nodded Resnick. "I think it's high time you dismantled this nonsensical device.'' He rocked his chair about violently as though he wanted to pitch it through the glass walls, smashing them and buckling the filigree cage for ever.

Ananda disagreed, however.

"It isn't a nonsensical device. No, I wouldn't say that. On the contrary! It amplifies the sense of death as something to experience. So it is a means, a pathway. Oh, it is most certainly the wrong path if you tread it in that direction — into the fantasy projections of your own mind. But perhaps it is the right path when you retrace your steps, back into yourself — and see yourself revealed as an illusion too.''

"Pretty words!'' snapped Alice. Yet Jim darted the man a glance of thanks — if indeed Ananda was trying to help him; and Jim believed that he was.

"Have you got any more Neo-H tablets?'' asked Resnick, sounding casual. Falsely casual.

"No,'' Jim lied. In fact there were half a dozen tablets in his pocket. He avoiding smoothing his coat down or doing anything similar to betray himself.

"I wonder,'' began Alice. But she was not wondering whether Jim was lying. "I wonder: Client Weinberger's vision of death has given him the glimpse of a path, as Lama Ananda says: a pathway through to safety and salvation. If Client Weinberger doesn't get 'captured' — if he dies 'surprised' — then he's safe. In his opinion! Right? So I wonder whether we should not, with his consent, arrange for him to die by surprise? For him not to know the moment? For it to come suddenly — as suddenly as a gunshot? We might make a bargain, Noel. If Client Weinberger will make public atonement — arrange his peace with the world — then later, at some time unknown except to . . .'' She hesitated.

"Except to Dr Menotti?'' asked Sally sharply.

103

Alice shook her head. "Ordinary euthanasia is too 'slow'."

"Except to the assassin," said Resnick bluntly. "Who would that be? Jim? Yourself? Will you, Alice, leap out pointing a gun and pull the trigger?"

"Where is the gun, by the way?" asked Alice.

"I handed it over to a Peace Officer," Jim told her. "I was close to Weinberger at the ceremony. Everyone else seemed paralysed."

"You *do* have a lot to do with all this. You didn't, by any chance, bring the gun from Gracchus in the first place, to slip into Weinberger's paw?"

"Don't be absurd!"

"So the gun's locked up in the Octagon. That's a shame. Perhaps."

"We can't start shooting people," said Resnick faintly. "What sort of good death would that be?"

" 'If any word of this got out,' " sneered Alice.

"Frankly, you sound like an *agent provocateur*, even to suggest it," Jim said gladly to the woman.

Alice inclined her head his way.

"Oh, very clever. Now you all listen to me. Weinberger won't die, except by surprise. We'll take that as read. So if that's his idea of a good death, well, why shouldn't we in this one instance oblige?"

"It could be interpreted as revenge," Ananda pointed out mildly. "Tit for tat."

"Oh, but *I* don't put forward any claim to do the deed. I'll tell you who ought to do it by any natural logic. Noel already named him as the prime candidate — and that's Weinberger's own trustworthy guide, the same guide who nursed that man's fantasies into full bloom!"

"Once it has bloomed, the flower can wilt," said Ananda. "Not before."

Alice ignored Ananda's aphorism, if indeed it amounted to such.

"Since the guide in question seems to have swallowed this whole rigmarole," she went on, "you can bet that he would shoot straight and true! For his client's sake, he'd have to!"

"He would be setting a terrible precedent," said Resnick. "The role of guide as friendly mediator, and the role of the euthanaser should be kept quite distinct."

Jim flared up.

"*I* would be setting a precedent? Me? As though I even suggested this, let alone . . .! Phew. A precedent, indeed! Precedents! I'd say that we're all getting just a bit too bureaucratic hereabouts. The time was, when a man who had just been miraculously cured would have merited some kind of . . . oh well, never mind! Okay, he's still a murderer. And the time was, too, when even a murderer — who was out of his wits at the time of the killing — would have just been isolated from society till such time as he could be eased gently back . . ."

". . . on to the motorway of murder," Alice finished for him. "As though he only had a flat tyre that needed changing and patching up."

"Oh, aren't we a *Roman* society now?" Weinberger had compared the present world to ancient Egypt because of the new pyramids of death. But Egypt was the wrong comparison entirely. The ancient Egyptians had been obsessed with the *afterworld*, with the land of the living dead. Whereas nowadays . . . "That's it, isn't it? No Gods but the State — society. We retire when the time seems ripe. We compose our farewell ode, in rhyming couplets — because they're easier to write — and we climb into a hot bath accompanied by our faithful razor. As it were."

"You aren't suggesting, by any chance, that we're *all* murderers in this House?" asked Alice quietly.

"You certainly seem to want *me* to be an executioner, not a guide!"

It was a lame retort. Everyone, even Ananda, was staring at him as though he was some alien visitor disguised as a man.

"Dr Menotti is no executioner!" cried Sally Costello indignantly.

"We're simply *discussing* this, Jim," said Resnick evenly. "Perhaps you're unused to democratic decisions: the free play of opinion, after which one settles on a common course. Coming from a larger House, as you do." After a moment's thought, he added, "But yes, we *are* a Roman society. That's quite a neat comparison! And Norman Harper was our finest patrician. But there's one little difference. Nowadays everybody is equally a patrician."

Mention of the poet utterly riled Jim. A poem broke from his lips like a belch.

"The Aztecs did it with an axe,
The Romans with a razor.
We do it with a silver needle
— Needles take longer to go blunt!

"If he's a poet, then so am I. Equally, and democratically."
Resnick shook his head sadly.

"It seems you have little real feeling for the humane collective spirit."

"In my view," said Alice, "we have more pressing matters to discuss than literary criticism, or Mr Todhunter's qualifications as a poet."

"Ah yes," said Jim, "we have a killing to plan. All right. Very well. Bravo! I shall put it to Nathan Weinberger that we will give him the surprise of his own sweet life. In return for which he will compose a farewell oration for us. Or something of the sort. If that will please you, Alice. We all want to please you, don't we?"

"Jim," warned Resnick.

"Oh, I'm perfectly serious. Excuse me for feeling some slight resentment at not being allowed to carry out my duties as a guide — as I truly see them."

"You've been doing all right in other respects."

"Except for a few missed appointments."

"Except for."

"Let's get this heap of junk taken apart for starters, eh? Who'll give me a hand?"

"One of the attendants can see to that, Jim. I'll send someone down right after lunch."

"Ah, no public penance for me, then." Jim laughed. "Only for Nathan. My penance will be quite private. To pull the trigger at dead of night. If I can get the gun back!"

"I'll give you a note for the Peace Office. Take it down to the Octagon this afternoon. But beyond that, we don't know anything about this, remember."

"And more than Nathan will? Maybe the dead of night's too obvious. The dead of day might be more surprising."

"None of us *know*, Jim. That way, no precedent exists."

"Oh, now I see. I, who have no feeling for the humane collective spirit, will naturally be the kind of maverick who couldn't

106

possibly set a precedent.''

'Ideally,' he thought grimly, 'after shooting Nathan I should do the decent thing and turn the gun on myself! I should stick the barrel . . . somewhere . . . and end this chain of murder before it spreads any further like a replicating virus. Incidentally, where *do* I point the gun? At my forehead? Or stick it under my ribs? Shall I ask Nathan for advice? "Nathan, how did you know just what part of Norman Harper's anatomy to aim at? Wasn't it a little risky shooting him in the throat first, just because you hated his poems? Such a tiny target! Or were you just firing wild, and lucky?" '

"You'd better send two attendants down," Jim told Resnick. "This junk is bulky. I should know."

"The material still belongs to the client," pointed out Ananda, adopting the prim tone of a legal adviser.

Resnick rubbed his hands.

"Soon, it won't."

Jim nodded.

"No, he won't be needing it. Not any more."

Indeed he wouldn't be. Not while Jim had the hypno-tape and the pills. This cage was out of date already. Who wanted to cage Death, when you could follow Death home to its native haunts instead? Which they had done together — almost. The behaviour of any caged creature was usually quite different from its behaviour in the wild.

This gilded cage was quite irrelevant now. Weinberger was trapped in a cage labelled 'Room 203'. And Jim was being trapped too, by circumstances and intrigues. Let the House pull Weinberger's invention to pieces. It would reassure them. The important thing was for Jim — and Nathan — to escape from *their* cages.

"I wonder what life and death are like these days in China and Russia and other assorted places?" said Jim on impulse.

"You mean *former* places," Resnick corrected him. "I'd say: hot — from isotopes. Skinny, from starvation. Pocked, with plague — and as cratered as the Moon. Quiet, really quiet on the whole. You can't call those 'places', Jim. They've fallen off the map."

'And where else is off the map?' Jim wondered.

107

NINETEEN

JIM ACCOMPANIED RESNICK to his office, where the Master scrawled a very brief note on House stationery and tucked it into an envelope which he didn't bother to seal.

"Give this to Toni Bekker, at the Octagon."

Jim pocketed the envelope.

"Bekker, eh? I've met him."

"Oh have you really? Would you mind telling me how?"

"He was the officer I gave the gun to, at the ceremony."

"And he took time off to tell you his name?"

"No, it was when I went down to the Octagon to register. I happened to make some enquiries about Weinberger."

"Did you indeed?"

"I was shunted on to Officer Bekker. He'd been out to Weinberger's apartment. He thought it was some sort of sex pervert's den, with the cage and screens and whatnot."

Resnick snorted.

"A pervert's den is about the size of it, downstairs right now! Not a sex pervert's, though — a death pervert's."

"By the way, Bekker sent you his regards. I forgot to pass them on."

Resnick's eyes narrowed.

"You do get around, don't you, Jim? A couple of days in Egremont, and you know everyone in town, and you've even paid a visit to the afterlife. It would be a real shame to lose so versatile a guide."

"Look, I'm just trying to do my job. But I keep on feeling as though I've walked into a performance of Macchiavelli's *The Prince*. And no one has bothered to tell me my lines."

"Ah, innocence is the best shield for any man, I always say."

"I thought you usually said, 'If any of this gets out.' Alice seems to have put her finger on *that*." Disregarding Resnick's obvious anger, Jim ploughed on: "Any of what?"

"Damn your impertinence! You've been planted here, haven't you? By Gracchus? No, not by Gracchus — it goes further than that! Who are you really, Jim?"

"Huh? I'm Jim Todhunter, and I'm an ordinary guide, that's all."

"And yet you indulge in sly jibes at the very basis of society! We all heard you."

"I thought I heard *you* say something about the free play of opinion . . ."

"What's more, you wheedle your way in with Weinberger, who is our ultimate hot potato."

"But you asked me to . . . This is insane! You told me to guide him."

"Ah, I had to, didn't I? Who else was available? And so conveniently, too! Who else happened to arrive on the very day — and at the very hour! — when Weinberger was planning his big surprise for us? As though your arrival was a signal to him! Poor Norman, he was one of the most innocent men alive . . ."

"If innocence was *his* shield, then it certainly wasn't bullet-proof!" Jim hastily checked his tongue, but the harm was done.

"So Norman isn't good enough for you. But you'll hole up with that bastard Weinberger, and build his mad machine, and arrange for his miracle cure! How was *that* part engineered, eh? The cure's real all right, I'll give you that. *If* his illness was ever genuine in the first place!"

"Not genuine? This is crazy. If I was . . . what you're suggesting . . ."

"And what's that? What is it, eh? Come on, put a name to it. Define it."

"Well, some kind of special agent — or conspirator — who's trying to . . ."

"Go on, say it."

"To bring down our present society."

"Yes, and whose agent would that be?"

"I haven't the slightest idea!"

"It's often better that way. You can't betray anyone. Why did

109

you ask that question about Russia and China? No, that's a red herring — literally! How about the Church, eh Jim? Put the fear of death into people, and they'll pray! But who cares about the Church any more? Or is it some really secret group? The Rosicrucians? The Illuminati?

"*Control*: that's what it comes down to, isn't it? Power! Bring this society of ours down in ruins, and you'll need a goddam dictatorship to replace what we've got now! All that we've blessedly won after years of stress and fear! And what better way to bring this society down than to infect everyone with the fear of death? The old terror! Only a beast would do that! A devil!"

Jim stared at the Master, amazed. Resnick was raving. Yet there was a curious self-control to his ravings, which Jim noted with bewilderment. Ordinarily a stutterer shouldn't be able to rave . . . So this had to be a performance: a show put on for the benefit of someone elsewhere — some imaginary person who would presently hear Jim's report.

Meanwhile Resnick was trying to trap Jim into betraying his 'controllers', by such wild stabs in the dark. Alice Huron would have done it more subtly and surgically. But Resnick had taken it upon himself, in order to reassert his authority — his own mastership.

'And I thought Nathan was paranoid! Nathan's the sanest man I ever met. Except for Mike Mullen. And me, I suppose.'

Resnick was out of control — like an actor who had begun to shout off about his own problems in the middle of a play.

And he was waggling his hands while he sounded off, as if making signals to Jim. He was crossing himself, genuflecting, twisting his wrists, bending his fingers. It looked like a sort of upright epilepsy. Or else a code known only to initiates. Yes, that was it: a secret code. Unfortunately Jim had no idea what the correct response might be. He couldn't signal back.

There was only one possible explanation for Resnick's behaviour. The awful truth about the red creatures which preyed on souls was suspected — or even known for a fact — by some select group, with whom Resnick had links, and whose creature he was. Yes, a group of individuals somewhere in the hierarchy of the Houses! And they were desperate to suppress that truth, for if it got out, why, the whole society of good death must inevitably go

110

smash. The result could quite conceivably be the extinction of the human race in a new round of sudden violence, civil war, *missiles*. (Had the doomsday machine ever really been dismantled? Or was it simply in mothballs?)

Were those people — the Controllers, as Jim now thought of them — prepared to permit any number of souls to go to the crystal hells and purgatories in order to preserve the human race on Earth? The hidden Controllers could, of course, always arrange a surprise death for themselves . . . a death such as Norman Harper had died! But subtler, far less public.

The poet hadn't been one of those Controllers. He was an innocent. Resnick said so. Resnick hoped to become a Controller if he fielded this crisis. Having risen already to Mastership of a House, he had discovered another summit hitherto hidden from view by the peak of the House.

Puppets . . . and puppeteers . . . It might even be that what Weinberger had suggested was true: that the Death creatures could indeed influence the minds of those in power, and consequently the whole structure of society, to provide a smooth supply of peace-fully dying souls . . . Perhaps the Death creatures even repaid their minions, their puppets, with paradises after death or with free passage through to the white light — if the creatures could be trusted to keep their word. Or if they could give it in the first place.

But . . . only a very few people could ever join this privileged élite, and they had to be initiated into it very cautiously.

The first qualification for membership in the ranks of these secret controllers was to realize that they existed at all. Resnick knew that they existed, and he aspired to be one of them. But, as yet, he didn't realize that the secret truth they guarded was the very same one that Jim and Weinberger had stumbled on. Or maybe Resnick suspected it, and the suspicion was driving him crazy. That, and the fear that he was being tested for loyalty. Or for something beyond loyalty.

Weinberger's machine and Jim's apparent complicity in it must seem to Resnick like a cunning test! Out of the blue. And Resnick feared that he would fluff the test. Maybe Alice Huron was one of those secret controllers herself — and Resnick, her protégé, was hoping to join her on equal terms . . . Possibly, too, the Controllers competed behind the scenes. For power. Whatever else did people ever compete for? If Resnick failed Alice, she lost ground.

'That's as may be,' thought Jim. 'I've no way of knowing. All I can find out is about Death itself. That's my destiny.'

Looking disgusted and angry, Resnick slumped into his chair.

'If I was testing him, I would flunk him. That makes him very dangerous to me.'

Once again, Jim placed his hands firmly on Resnick's desk — realizing, as he did it, that this was an unfortunate move. It made Jim seem far more important, and knowledgeable, than he really was.

"I'm going to forget all about this . . . outburst, Noel." No doubt this was inappropriate too. "I'm just a guide, and I have a deal to offer to my client." Jim patted his pocket. "But first, I must visit the Octagon. So I guess I'll skip lunch."

"Hmm," said Resnick, presumably unable to decide whether Jim was declining a non-existent invitation tactfully, or pointedly.

Once outside the office, Jim doubled back down to the basement. In the midst of his grand gesture of condemning Weinberger's machine to the scrap heap he had forgotten something essential, though he had remembered to bring the cassette player from the blue room.

Crawling into the cage for what would be the last time, he disconnected the pheromone dispenser with its few remaining drams of the liquid which had already fooled Death twice. The attendants whom Resnick would send down shortly would have no way of knowing it had ever been part of the cage.

Jim regretted the loss of the 'thanatos' rhythm equipment. However, *its* absence would be noted, sooner rather than later. Besides, it was too bulky and it required a power source.

'We'll have to improvise,' he thought. 'We'll manage. Somehow.' He had already decided to put out of his mind, as much as was possible, the problem of Resnick, Alice, the Egremont House and the Controllers. That situation was perhaps resolvable if he did as they wanted him to, and executed Weinberger. On the other hand, maybe it wasn't. Maybe that course of action would lead inevitably to his own premature retirement. Keeping the 'scandal' under the firm wraps of the House, they could claim that

Jim had gone insane . . .

Whereas he felt particularly sane right now. After all, had he not caught a distant glimpse of the existence of hidden Controllers? Likewise he had almost caught a glimpse of the hidden roosting place of Death, beyond the prisons which awaited souls.

'Maybe I can't quite cope with the intrigues . . . but I can cope with Death. That's my adventure.'

Jim took the elevator back up to his own room, and stowed the player and the corpse sweat dispenser in his valise. The yucca leaves outside the window clustered menacingly, suggesting to him the ripping open of his bag — which reminded him about the unread note in his pocket, which did not need to be slit or steamed to open it. He took it out.

The note which he was to carry to the Octagon consisted of just four words:

Give him the thing.

It was not signed, only initialled, though presumably Resnick's scrawl was unmistakable. The Master's letters looped childishly in the same way as he himself was given to performing figure-of-eight gyrations of the body. Otherwise, perhaps, his writing would have stuttered into illegibility . . .

Jim stared at the note, more amused than bemused.

Give him the thing.

The note was a blank cheque. It seemed incredible that anyone would hand over a lethal weapon on the basis of such a flimsy hint, even to a guide from the House of Death. Oh, how the note smacked of pre-arrangement — even though Resnick had appeared to be so strongly opposed to Alice's seemingly spontaneous suggestion. At first.

Yes, there were Controllers — and apprentice Controllers: those whose loyalty to the system must be tested, at the expense of an occasional client, or guide . . .

'What the hell,' thought Jim. Whom a gun hit depended on whom it was pointed at. Better to be holding it, than not! Metaphorically, of course. He would never contemplate actually using a gun. Perhaps Nathan would, but Nathan was somewhat risky in that area. Unreliable.

Or maybe devilishly reliable!

Slipping the note back into his pocket, Jim set off for the

Octagon. He whistled to himself.

'The die is cast,' he thought. Die? Yes, it all came down to the gamble of dying . . .

Yet, as he walked, despite his decision to keep his mind clear for other things, he went over his puzzling encounter with Resnick once more.

What the hell *was* going on in Egremont? Involving Resnick and Alice and Officer Bekker and Death knows who else?

If only he could put his finger on the exact source of Resnick's apparently paranoid fugue . . . He almost felt that the source was . . . himself. But that was ridiculous. How could *he* be blamed for what Resnick said and imagined? The truth of it was that Resnick was about to have a nervous breakdown. Resnick had been riding high, preening himself. Resnick had been looking forward to rewards for his successful rule of the House. Then Norman Harper had been murdered, terrifying him.

And unfortunately, even though there were checks and balances in any House, the ultimate power of life and death was in Resnick's hands. Power over everyone, including Jim.

'The *ultimate* power of Death?' Jim chuckled bitterly to himself. How little Resnick knew. Or any of them. Only Jim and Nathan knew. Only they had chased Death, almost to its home.

Secret political intrigues were going on, he decided, but there couldn't really be a group anywhere in the House hierarchy who knew the truth about Death. If such a group existed, and they continued to operate the Houses, it would be too evil for words. Resnick believed that he was being led into temptation — for political gain. So he would deliver himself from the evil of the bait. By any means.

But other people wouldn't. Others would listen. Surely. Possibly.

Jim's shoes crunched the gravel as he crossed the courtyard to the Octagon; which prompted him to wonder about their staying power over rougher terrain. But he could not really feel the stone chips through the rubber soles, so he supposed that the shoes would serve.

He checked in at the front desk. The same white-uniformed woman was on duty. Presently he accompanied another messenger

114

up to Bekker's office.

"So it's you again," said Bekker, in an unwelcoming way.

Jim slid the envelope across Bekker's desk.

"He did send me, this time," said Jim deviously.

Bekker removed the note, scanned it in a moment then turned the paper over as though some explanation or endorsement might be written on the back. But no: Bekker was simply placing the sheet of paper face down so that it was indeed a blank sheet. The message no longer existed. He had never seen it.

Without a word Bekker got up, went to a wall safe and removed a small package which he handed to Jim. Jim weighed it, and dropped it into his pocket.

Sitting down again, Bekker smiled for the first time.

"What a beautiful day," he said. Since his window glass was opaque this seemed a doubly hypocritical remark. "Nice of you to drop by."

"But you're so very busy."

"Right. Alas."

Bekker smiled again, and Jim departed, to ride the Beadway back to the House like a mugger of old with a murder weapon hidden in his pocket.

TWENTY

". . . So we've got to get out of here, Nathan."

"I see. You really think the pheromone flask and the hypno-tape will be enough?"

"They'll have to be. We aren't in the butterfly trapping game any longer. It's just a question of getting our timing right, transferring into our second bodies, then giving chase. But we can't do that from here any longer — cage or no cage."

Leaning to one side, Weinberger dialled a succession of new scenes for the wall screen: a cactus desert, cumulus cloud islands detached from any land beneath, ripe cornfields with not a bird in sight. He ended up with the rolling forests which he had been gazing at when Jim first met him.

"We used to go hiking when I was younger. I knew the ground north of here up as far as Barnaby. There were forest retreats, with

115

rations kept in them. Used to be. Still will be, I suppose. Of course, the Peace Service know where those all are. But there are other places in the woods and hills. Old mines, fishing cabins, firetowers. I must say I feel a lot stronger, though I don't know what shape I'm in for hiking. Lying around in bed can't have helped! Still . . . We are going north, aren't we?''

''We'll take a car, to give us a start. If the battery's fully charged, we'll make thirty-five or forty miles before it runs out of juice. Then we'll hide the car.''

''Leaving approximately another hundred miles to the border — and over that border, other Houses of Death.''

''Run by different people, with different political pressures operating on them. Maybe there'll be less hidden manoeuvring. They're supposed to be more free and easy up there.''

''So is Egremont supposed to be. I'm still an absconding murderer, remember. I killed Cock Robin. I shot the poet laureate.''

''We'll have tracked Death to its lair, by then. We'll have gone beyond the crystal prisons. We'll have news. Since Egremont won't listen, that's why we ran to them.''

''Not ran, Jim — walked. Quite slowly. Hoping that they'll listen to us. Why should they want to?''

''Because it's the truth.''

Weinberger sighed. ''You don't really quite believe that yet, do you? Despite what we went through together. Your mind's still running on two separate tracks. One, what we experienced was real. Two, it was a fantasy. You're getting out of here for reasons of your own. Involving your own skin.''

''That's true too,'' admitted Jim. ''But even so. You know, they'll expect me to head back towards Gracchus to hole up in the city. So we'll be safe heading north.''

''Safe as Houses. Speaking of safety, I once told you that a hydrogen bomb might be the best defence against Death because it vapourizes people before they know it. Do you remember? I was talking rather wildly.''

''Indeed you were.''

''But I've thought since, what about all the casualties who die slowly from burns and radiation? My real point is, what can anyone *do* about Death, if it's the truth? Which it is. Do they retrain all the guides as a guild of assassins — sudden killers gliding through society, picking off this man here and that woman there before he or she ever suspects a thing? In cahoots with the Census Office and the Peace Service? Oh, that would really turn the world upside-down! Though I guess it already has been turned upside-down once in my lifetime, so I suppose anything is possible. Oh, but you'd need a Norman Harper and a half to versify that regime!

> "Death comes from the blue
> It comes to me, it comes to you,
> A rifle bullet from a tower,
> Today, tomorrow, any hour.
> Death doesn't catch any of you.
> *We* do."

"That's why we need more information," said Jim. "We have to trail Death to its lair."

"In the woods, in the hills. Well, I don't suppose we have any choice about it — and I'm glad to hear you convincing yourself."

Jim slapped his pocket.

"If they pick up *our* trail, we can defend ourselves."

"With just six shots left?"

"We can pretend to. Nobody argues with a gun. By the way, I meant to ask you: how do you best use it? If 'best' is the right word! I don't mean how do you pull the trigger — that's obvious — nor do I intend to! Just —"

Weinberger thumped his own chest. "A fellow's heart is over here. And you don't *pull* the trigger, Jim. You squeeze it. Or you'll miss. And don't forget that there's a safety catch — or that a gun kicks. Not," he added sarcastically, "that you'll be using it."

"You'd better believe it. One other thing — hypothetically, you understand? Purely as a matter of interest."

"Well?"

"How would someone go about shooting *himself*? Would he hold the gun backwards, like this?" Pointing both hands back towards his heart, Jim mimed.

"You try that when you're holding a gun, and you'll find how easy it isn't. No way." Weinberger stuck his index finger into his mouth, then pulled it out with a plop. "That's how. Pointing upwards, or you'll just blow the back of your throat out. I think that's how. Hell, it's all so long ago."

"In your case, about ten days ago!"

"I mean all the information about killing. The serials, the soap operas. Look, Jim, this conversation's getting a little muddle-headed. Either you're planning on taking to the hills with me — or on shooting me. Not both at once."

Jim raised a hand in protest.

"No, what I'm wondering is: can you ever shoot yourself by surprise — if you do it quickly and impulsively enough?"

"How do I know? Do you think I want to put it to the test? What I'd say is, that nobody ever commits suicide on impulse. So it's a fool question. But you've got one thing right. Our job's to stay alive — and we won't manage it here."

Weinberger gazed into the scene-screen.

"I'd better get rid of that. Forests are a dead give-away. It's a pity there aren't any city scenes!"

Weinberger dialled the forests away, and the winter of the world faced them once again, glazed by the flood of sunlight reflecting off the icebergs.

"We'll leave tomorrow night," said Jim. "I'll tell Resnick that you're on the verge of agreeing to appear in public."

"And I *will* so appear. Only, no one will be up and about to see me. Thus proving that a part of the truth is the biggest lie of all. Oh, that's neat. I shall eat like a horse till then."

"In that case, *bon appetit* to you."

"No, I'll just eat like a horse, that's all."

TWENTY-ONE

WHEN THE TIME came, Jim opened the door to the monitor room softly. Sorensen sat with his back to the door, reading his eternal magazine. On the little screen a tiny Weinberger lay on his bed studiously ignoring the camera eye and whatever might transpire behind it.

Sorensen looked round and saw the gun in Jim's hand.

"Don't make a sound," said Jim. "Don't touch anything.

Don't move. Or you'll be dead — by murder." He closed the door behind him.

Sorensen moved rather more than previously. He shook.

"If you shoot me, it'll make a noise!"

"And that'll be the noise of your own death. But you won't hear it."

"You're crazy. You're fucking crazy."

"That's as may be. If you don't do exactly what I tell you, you'll be on the receiving end of my craziness. And I just told you to *shut up*!"

Why did he have to speak to the man? Jim felt that he should be just grunting or barking at him. He resented the absurd melodrama. Worse, holding up a man at gunpoint felt like suddenly having a big glass ball or soap bubble balanced in mid-air. Once up, you couldn't put it down or it would break under its own weight. Once begun, the thing wouldn't go away.

"Don't do this, Mr Todhunter, sir! Just because I called in Mr Resnick? I had to do that."

"Shut up." The glass ball was making too much noise. "If you do what I tell you, I won't kill you." Jim felt like an oversized child playing at some adult activity which he only half understood. He waved the gun.

"Pull your chair over by the wall — next to that pipe."

Sorensen began jumping his chair towards the pipe while still sitting on it — which caused an almighty scraping and screeching.

"Lift it, you fool! Just off the floor, no higher. Now set it down. And catch this."

Jim produced a fat roll of adhesive tape, which he tossed to the man. Sorensen fumbled the catch. The tape rolled away across the floor.

Keeping his gun on the man, Jim retrieved the tape and rolled it back in the direction of Sorensen's feet.

"Right, pick it up. Open it. Now tape your mouth shut. Good. Next, tape your ankles to the chair legs . . .

"Right, now tape your left arm to the chair arm."

This was not as easy as it sounded, but eventually Sorensen succeeded in binding his left wrist. The tape roll hung loose; Sorensen couldn't tear the perforations with one hand. He mumbled through his gag apologetically.

Jim edged over to him. He removed the tape roll and bound Sorensen's right wrist quickly, cursorily. Then he put the gun down on the floor and methodically began to retape his prisoner's mouth, wrists and ankles firmly till he had used up all the tape. He produced cord and bound the man. Next, he tipped the chair back carefully till Sorensen was lying like an astronaut of old, waiting for lift-off, and he knotted the chair to the pipe. Waiting for lift-off by an angry Resnick . . .

"Mmm-mmm," said Sorensen. Uncomfortable? Pipe too hot? Blood running to his head?

Jim wondered whether he should bang Sorensen on the head with the gun butt, but he had no idea how hard to hit him. Or how softly. He contented himself with threatening him.

"Shut up. I'm going to be here behind you quite a while, and I don't want to hear a peep — or I'll hit you on the head. And that might bust your skull!"

He removed the key to the rear door of the House and left silently, retrieving his packed valise from outside the room.

When Jim had checked the front foyer of the House earlier on a woman attendant had been sitting there, teasing coloured threads into a half-embroidered sampler. It was a picture of a sperm whale sounding in the open ocean. Apparently she was going to be there all night. Jim hoped that the woman and Sorensen weren't lovers, in the habit of phoning each other or paying sneak visits. But why should they be? Not everyone loved everybody else.

Really, it was a nuisance that he had needed to immobilize the spy Sorensen. But, key aside, the man couldn't be trusted to respect a request for all-night privacy. Not any longer. And at least the exercise of mastering the man at gunpoint — despite the gaucherie of it — had given Jim confidence.

An hour later an electric runabout toiled up over the ridge separating Lake Tulane from Egremont. A half moon and cold stars lit the scene faintly in blue: not so much a light as a lessening of darkness. The headbeams picked out the winding road for a little way ahead, and washed against the trees. Behind, the valley was an empty bowl, its pearly spider's-web of lights extinguished some time ago.

Jim glanced at his watch, but couldn't read it in the instant during which he dared take his eyes off the road. He knew the time, anyway: shortly after midnight.

"Turn right here." Weinberger, pencil light in hand, spotted a little yellow circle of lines and symbols upon the otherwise black map sheet. The map would be some help in getting them smoothly away from Egremont, then of increasingly little use as they tried to lose themselves so successfully that nobody else could find them either. So it was a map for getting lost by.

Shortly after the turn-off, Jim glanced through an opening in the trees and thought that he recognized, though from a different angle, the chalet by the waters where trout had been grilled to celebrate his arrival. A light showed down there. If Noel Resnick was sporting in the chalet with Mary-Ann and Alice while Jim and Weinberger slipped by, this indeed added spice to their escape!

But why should it be Resnick with his ladies? Maybe it was a different chalet entirely, sheltering some solitary yachtsman afflicted with insomnia . . .

'I'm obsessed with sex,' thought Jim grimly. 'But I haven't been to bed with anyone. Only with Weinberger, inside his contraption, and that doesn't count. Is Death my only real sexual encounter, of which all the others are mere echoes and shadows? Is the real act of conception not the engendering of a child in the womb but the fertilisation of one of those crystal prisons by my soul? So here go I, like a self-denying monk, an obsessed St Anthony, into the desert to triumph over that crystal temptation — or succumb to it . . .

'Yes, I'm a monk.' He had been sleeping in his coffin or close by it for years now. The House of Death was the coffin that they all lived in. Yet how the others enjoyed themselves in it! How everybody enjoyed themselves now that they all knew how to die . . .

'Except for me.' Somewhere, somehow, he had lost out on enjoyment. Maybe it was when he drowned. The joy of that drowning had been so much more intense than any subsequent drowning in the flesh of another . . .

"We stay on this route." Weinberger whispered, as though sensing his reverie and not wanting to interrupt it but at the same time wishing to be part of it.

The metalled road became pocked and bumpy. The electric runabout lurched on at twenty-five miles per hour, its top speed.

* * *

121

A little over an hour later the engine began to fade.

By now they were bumping along a forest road which seemed to be proceeding satisfactorily from nowhere to nowhere, though generally northwards. They had already passed off the edge of the local map. Losing the car might not, however, be so simple. Black fir trees hemmed the road.

Clouds covered the half moon which only occasionally floated clear, a phosphorescent bone. Jim slowed, to hunt for a crack in the darkness of the forest. He had imagined that they might come across a deep little lake with water like oil, and scuttle the car in it. But now he had no means of telling whether there was such a lake fifty yards away, let alone any hope of reaching it on wheels.

Finally he found something wider than a crack and swung the runabout hard into it. Branches scraped the windows. A tree stub screeched across the underside. The wheels spun, and the engine died. Both men had to force their way out through the driver's door. A needle-studded branch slapped Jim across the cheek.

"Nobody might come along for days," said Weinberger encouragingly.

And thus they set off along the road.

Five minutes later, Jim shifted his valise to his left hand. Five minutes after that he tried hanging the bag over his shoulder; and another five minutes later he thought of wearing it on his back, rucksack style, with his arms through the handles. But this cramped his shoulders, and the bag butted his spine. He returned it to his right hand.

Presently they arrived at the top of a great clearing. Felled trees cascaded down the hillside like matchsticks spilled from a box. A log cabin crowned the rise, dark and empty. The road ran nowhere else.

"My arm's two yards long," Jim complained.

"Well, we can't stop here. We've only come a couple of miles!"

Aided rather more, now, by the glowing bone in the sky, they struck off and up into the wild.

To Jim's surprise, Weinberger had reserves of strength. It was as though the man had converted all the pain dealt out by the creature Death into some honey-energy in his body cells. Now the terrain was rougher, but this very roughness was a help to them since reefs of rock broke through the forest, parting the trees. After half an hour Weinberger allowed them to halt in the lee of a junior crag. He sank down.

"I'm pooped."

Jim dropped his leaden valise, which had fused his fingers together.

"I've been sleepwalking."

"Okay, let's sleep."

"Where?" Jim peered into the night.

"It's quite easy in theory. Animals do it all the time. You just lie down, curl up and go to sleep."

"Oh, you funny fellow."

From his bag Jim pulled the two lightweight capes which he had bought that morning. He spread them on the ground. Weinberger shuffled on to one of them and made a pillow of his arms. Jim copied him, worrying about how crumpled their clothes would look by the time they crossed the border. That border was still immeasurably far off; it felt like a whole country away.

The tussocky ground wasn't too hard, but a chill clung to it which Jim hadn't noticed while they were walking. After a while, hesitantly he fitted himself right up against Weinberger, who appeared to be asleep already. He tucked his buttocks into the other man's belly and folded the hollows of his knees around the other man's knees. Before, in Egremont, they had been Sleeping Beauties; now they were the Babes in the Wood. Creaky old babes.

TWENTY-TWO

JIM WAS STILL wondering how he would ever get to sleep, when he realized that it was already daylight.

He had dreamt troubled, wakeful dreams: complicated, guilty racings of the mind upon the theme of how to switch off those same racings. There existed a maze of switches to do this. As soon as he threw one switch, though, this gave birth to a whole subsidiary maze. Eventually mazes and switches towered to the sky.

And that sky was now bright with the morning sun. He blinked, wondering where all that complex of apparatus had gone to. Surely it couldn't have packed itself back into his skull? But it had; and he had spent his hours of sleep like a rat in some old torture laboratory, which happened to be his own brain.

Weinberger had gone. Jim sat up in dizzy panic. A bird — but he was not very good on birds, so that it was simply 'a bird' — twittered on a branch then flew off suddenly as Weinberger came up through the pines back to the crag.

Weinberger sniffed the air appreciatively.

"Lovely morning, Jim. Good to be alive, as they say."

Jim shook his head, to clear it of the last switches and mazes. He sniffed the air too — it was like a cool green drink — and he sneezed. Twice, three times, explosively.

Weinberger chuckled.

"Cut it out. You don't catch cold from lying on the ground. Cold is a virus."

Jim shivered, and sneezed again.

"Stop it!"

Amazingly, Jim did stop sneezing.

"When did you wake up?"

"I told you: I don't use much sleep. I've been scouting. There's a spring down there — fully certified for washing and drinking. Freshen up, take a leak, and we'll open one of those cans you brought. Oh, it's just like the old days — give or take a tent. And a fire. We can't light any fires up here. No fire without smoke. Go on, lazybones, *git*! I let you sleep in this morning."

Jim groaned, and massaged his legs.

At mid-day, when they had covered another six or seven miles, they stopped to open another can and eat some chocolate. Both men were ravenous, and Jim realized that the groceries he had brought would hardly last through the next day. When Jim mentioned this, Weinberger airily reminded him that he intended to catch fish with the line and hook he had told Jim to buy. He promised a feast of edible fungi too, which would taste like steaks — and be topped with sweet blackberries. But Jim saw only spruce and pine, grass and sky.

They sat on a spruce-clad ridge, eating. The breeze was very fresh, despite the continuing sunshine. A squirrel scampered up a tree and sat watching them intently, clutching some trophy in its paws, ready to dart to the far side of the trunk. Steep green valleys lay ahead — and somewhere in the distance a thin waterfall tumbling from its crag into a hidden lake or pool.

Hearing a buzz in the sky, they took shelter behind the squirrel's tree, sending it leaping to another.

A mile westward a white monoplane flew into view. It veered this way and that. It circled.

"Peace Service plane," remarked Weinberger. "So that means they've found the runabout, and the cone of search points this way. Can't win 'em all! But that's a hopeless way of looking for someone. They'd be lucky to spot us even if we were up a tree waving a red sheet at them."

Gradually the monoplane moved away.

Later, a second monoplane passed almost directly overhead, then swung back towards the north-east. This one had wing-tip floats instead of wheels.

"That's from Barnaby," said Weinberger. "Hence the floats. That's because of all the lakes they've got over there. It was just a coincidence passing over us like that. They didn't see a thing."

"If they do see us —"

"They'll drop officers in by parachute, the same as they do for fires." Weinberger scanned the horizon. By now it had gone into mourning with black crepe along it beneath white cauliflower domes. "Don't worry. The weather's going to foul up in another hour or two. Let's reach a lake. Our supper ought to be able to tell the difference between a few raindrops and a wriggly worm."

A few raindrops. This was sheer bravado. When it did start to rain steadily a couple of hours later, with grey clouds dredging along below the tops of the slopes, both men were soon soaked through and shivering despite their capes. When they finally did arrive at a lakeside, the lake seemed like a mere local thickening of the water which already filled the air.

Though partly occupied with feeling miserable, Jim had nevertheless — under the lash of the rain — managed to track down a certain quality of, call it, inattention about their escape into the forests. They had brought food along, yes, and a fishing line, and a couple of capes; and so on. But they were just not geared up for a trek to the border. Therefore *they were not really going there*. He understood this now, while the rain dripped off him, and through him. The border was an alibi, a lie. They had paced themselves for a sprint, not a marathon. It was all they were good for: a sprint lasting two or three days at the most . . .

'Give us two or three days, and we'll damn well prove we're right!' As to afterwards, why, the non-existent Gods could see to that. Or Justice, or Fate, or even, incredibly, Truth. Unconsciously, they had made this bargain: this magical, infantile bargain.

Jim found himself remembering an old German poem in favour with the Houses: Friedrich Hölderlin's *To the Fates*. More accurately, Norman Harper's version of it was in favour. But out of curiosity Jim had once accessed the original back in Gracchus. The original petitioned the Fates to grant another summer and another autumn of life to ripen the poet's song. To Jim's ear the German original sounded very hectoring, but Norman Harper's 'translation' was something of a misrepresentation, to say the least . . .

Norman Harper called his version *Windfall*. It was another of his rare departures from a rhyme scheme. Jim whispered the 'translation' to himself sourly, trying to remember the bargaining German voice that lay hidden beneath Harper's verses like some buried Troy.

'Will you let me fade in the Fall,
My kindly Powers That Be?
My poems will be ripe for plucking,
Heart's pollen will be all sweet honey
For the next year's folk.

'Hullo there, Stillness, how are you?
I'm goodly glad, even if I'm not to hear
My own voice versing any more.
In my own way I've lived like Goethe.
But you know, apples overripe go rotten . . .

'Why don't you pick my windfall, now?'

Which would have been all very well, and autumny, earlier in the day when the sun was still shining! But of course, it was a different kind of bargain that Norman Harper was intent on striking. Harper bargained not with the Fates, but with the State. Not for a little more lease of life, but for a good death. It was the Hölderlin sort of bargain that they were into now: for a few more hours of freedom, to produce something.

Jim shook water out of his hair.

"We're going to chase Death home soon," he said. "All we need is somewhere to shelter. Nobody can creep up on us in this weather. Afterwards — we'll see."

Weinberger nodded wetly, like a dog after a swim. He seemed to share Jim's feelings about the journey. They were heading towards a different border entirely, and over it, and back again, with the truth, with evidence. That was their real journey, not this farce of a hike.

"I think that's a hut over on the other side, isn't it?"

They peered across this lake, into which the sky melted.

A quarter mile away as the crow flies a little shack hunched vaguely. A mile or more around the banks of the kidney-shaped waters. It would be a kennel to dry off in.

It took half an hour of slipping and sliding and detouring to reach the shack.

Inside, piled in a corner, were two delapidated mattresses with their stuffing coming out. Empty, cobwebbed shelves lined one wall. The roof leaked in a few places, and there was no glass in the single window that overlooked the rain-lashed waters. But here was shelter, and even a sort of luxury. A three-legged chair lay toppled on the floorboards; its fourth leg had walked off elsewhere long ago.

Jim broke the chair up and began to scavenge anything else that would burn. He prised the shelves loose. He pulled up a broken floor plank, then another — their nails as loose as a radiation victim's teeth. He scooped dry earth from under the hut to serve as a fire base, and began to splinter wood. He discovered a pile of yellowed old magazines under a sack. They would light the splinters, which would light the larger pieces of wood.

Faithful to his promise of fish for supper, Weinberger went out into the rain again with the hook and line.

Jim's clothes were steaming on his body beside a decent fire when the other man came back twenty minutes later. The smoke billowed out of the window, losing itself in the smoke of rain.

Weinberger winked broadly. From behind his back he jerked out a sagging speckled trout, its mouth wide open in horrid surprise.

"Three pounds, if it's an ounce!"

Weinberger gutted the fish, spitted it on a stick and handed this to Jim to cook.

"Pity we haven't a quart of whisky with us!"

Even without whisky they feasted royally, burning their fingers. Then they dragged the mattresses closer to the dying fire, as the day too — already submerged by rain — drowned through dusk into darkness.

TWENTY-THREE

THE NEXT MORNING dawned wet and gloomy; which encouraged them. Land, lake and sky had all run together now into one amorphous whole, as though the world was returning to some primitive state of being.

Since there was no more ready wood to scavenge, Jim opened a can of corned beef to eat cold. When they had emptied it turn by turn, Weinberger set the empty can out under the eaves to catch rainwater.

Using the fishing line, Jim slung the pheromone drip flask from a nail in the roof within easy reach of the two mattresses; then he checked the battery power of the cassette player. He tapped out two of the orange hearts of Neo-Harmaline-MDA from a twist of paper. By his watch it was seven-thirty.

Presently Weinberger ducked out to fetch the can, which now held a finger of rain. Jim would rather have swallowed his own pill dry, but there was something ceremonial about the way in which Weinberger toasted him then shoved the can his way; so he washed his pill down with the remaining ounce of meat-flavoured gruel.

Fully dressed on this occasion, they stretched themselves upon the musty mattresses. Jim reached out; Mike Mullen's voice began to drone.

Later — but how much later, he had no idea — his hand remembered to touch the pheromone tap.

Later — or was it earlier? — as the shack was revealed for the ghost of a shack that it was, he floated up towards the rickety roof along with Weinberger. The grey wet air outside, and inside too, was more cloud than air: a luminous cloud contaminated with dirty shadows. The shadows of the trees backing away from the lake; the shadows of the ordinary world.

Jim gazed down upon the motionless bodies of two hobos, who might be dead of exposure on their filthy mattresses. But he watched those makeshift corpses with a sense of rapture. It was the old rapture of drowning into oceanic light — a light which he now knew to be split by a billion crystal prisms, prisons which reproduced themselves by fission to garner yet more souls.

And because he was simply out of his body, and not actually dead, the ordinary world still cast strong shadows to distract him from that contaminated light. The shadows of the forest pulled at him, urging him to haunt the woodlands, and even to skim back to Egremont. He bobbed like a balloon, caught between the shadow wind and a different breeze that blew towards the white fog.

Death appeared suddenly, a red fire upon those hobos' chests. From waxwork Jim to waxwork Weinberger it hopped back and forth.

This time, they navigated the fog with its coloured crystals more speedily. From side to side they arced, tight on Death's tail.

Sometimes quite wide straits opened out between the crystals, straits down which Death flew. Sometimes there was far less room for manoeuvre. Yet still the crystals stretched on and on in all directions, apparently forever: a great ocean in which chunks of coloured ice of the same density as water floated at all levels. It was a maze of many possible pathways and innumerable cul-de-sacs — Death's dead ends — which they could never have picked their way through on their own. Surely a boundary must exist, a brighter or a clearer light beyond . . . but where it might be it was impossible to tell, or set one's course by, so broken up and so refracted was that true light by the crystal fog.

Death did not exactly ignore them on this occasion. The further into the fog that they chased it, the more it seemed to react to their pursuit by sudden hoverings and pivotings and by quick backward glances, its ruby eyes glittering like crystals in miniature. Death did not seem angry that they were chasing it. Or afraid. Nor did it try to shake them off by squeezing along narrow paths. Rather, it seemed to be luring them on now — keeping ahead of them, but never too far ahead.

Jim wondered how far their elastic life-lines could really stretch. Would the silver threads reach snapping point? Then would Death sweep back to gather them? For all he knew, Death was leading them cunningly in circles . . .

"Is there no end to it?" called Weinberger.

But then, quite suddenly, there was an end. They were through. Out they darted on Death's tail between the final crystals — into a lucid, shining emptiness which was very like a negative of space: a white void. It was lit, yet from no particular source other than itself. Now there was only the red creature ahead of them, flying unimpeded.

Behind, the crystal fog was a wall which divided this universe in half. Breaking out of the fog, Jim had felt that he had been . . . 'unconceived'. They were two sperms leaving that enormous egg of a myriad coloured cells. Or was it more like glassy cuckoo spit?

The wall receded as they flew away from it into the white void. It hardly seemed to grow much smaller to a backward glance, only smoother — smooth as a billiard ball. But yes, there was a slight curvature to it now. It was an enormous sphere.

And it was the home of a myriad mind-worlds, and a billion soul-imaginings — including many purgatories and hells. Whilst out here there was simply a bright nothingness . . . Jim began to fear a greater peril, that of being cast adrift by Death in limbo. Was this void the same as Ananda's 'pure Nothing'? No, since it contained light. He could see, though there was nothing to be seen. He knew he was conscious, though there was very little to be conscious of.

"Where are we?" cried his companion.

"Watch Death, Nathan! Don't take your eyes off Death!"

Apart from the tiny red speeding creature, there was only a blank visual field. If Death, indeed, was still speeding . . . Perhaps it was standing still, and so were they.

Like any single item concentrated on relentlessly for too long, the red creature was becoming meaningless. Their eyes would soon blank it out, their brains would not register it, and it would vanish too. They would lose it.

By now Jim's mind was willing the blank void *to be something*. His eyes hunted for any marbling or mottling or grain in the luminous space: for some sort of texture or irregularity. Soon, what had seemed at first like indefinite extension ahead and above and beneath them seemed more like . . . walls. Yes, there was a spherical wall behind them: that was the crystal fog. Why should there not be walls ahead too? No space could be utterly unbounded, extending forever. Even a universe must bend back upon itself, so that it created out of itself its own walls: Moebius strip walls with no other side but this one side. The void, too, must bend back upon itself . . .

Now they were indeed flying through an enormous room, with the most peculiar walls: they were at once everywhere, and nowhere. The enormous room was nothing less than an infinity of 'local' rooms, coexisting within one and the same space. Bring one room into focus out of this infinity — choose it — and there you would be. No longer in infinity; and yet on the other side of its walls, its one-sided walls, there would still be all the other possible rooms and spaces. Here was a place that was infinite, yet bounded. No 'elsewhere' existed — only an eternal *here*: the quality of being here, yet with access to everywhere.

Within the crystal fog that they had left behind, trapped souls also chose the shape of their world-spaces — of their rooms — modelling them on their dreams and fears. Yet those lost souls were all separated from each other forever. Whereas this 'room' was the Many-in-One. It allowed infinite access.

As Jim realized this, and chose *something*, the room took on architecture, texture, furnishings . . .

It became a long rococo hall. He and Weinberger were walking along it now, together. Red Death flew on ahead of them down to the furthest end.

The two men took stock of their surroundings.

The floor was of polished parquet. A number of gilded chairs and brocaded sofas stood about, and several round tables the tops of which were inlaid with strips of contrasting marble. The roof was of many linked domes, painted to resemble blue skies with fleecy clouds. The richly papered, embossed walls were subdivided into alcoves or little antechambers each of which housed a closed

131

double door with moulded covings above it and a carved head-piece: of cherubs, tritons, centaurs, bunches of grapes in gilded wood. All along this hall, reaching up to the false sky, was intricacy: carved gilded wreaths, cartouches, friezes, architraves. Nowhere were there windows; yet outside each alcove there hung a heavy ornamental picture frame, and though no painting was inside a single one of these — only a blank space — somehow these seemed to illuminate the hall. With a one-way light: one couldn't see where it came from, only what it fell upon within this place.

Death had dipped into an alcove at the very end of the hall and settled there, clinging upside-down to the headpiece of the furthest door.

Keeping an eye open for any flicker of movement on its part, just in case it darted back towards them, Jim strode to the door closest by. He gripped the curled, gold handles and pulled the twin doors open . . .

TWENTY-FOUR

A BEECHWOOD GREW outside, the trees smooth and tapering with the only foliage up at the roof of the wood. The ground was a lavender mist of bluebells. A path led through the wood, disappearing from sight.

Erect on its hind legs, a shaggy wolf with a long thin snout leaned idly against one of the beeches. It panted, pink-tongued. And its teeth dripped saliva. Yet it held a posy of bluebells in one of its forepaws. It looked as though it had only stopped running and adopted this nonchalant pose a moment earlier.

Shrugging itself off the tree, the wolf strolled towards them, holding out the bunch of flowers, grinning wetly, invitingly. Hastily Jim slammed the doors.

"Open up again," said Weinberger.

"Huh?"

"Just an idea. Go on."

Cautiously Jim opened the doors a crack, then pulled them wide. Now there was no bluebell wood outside. In its place was a moated castle set in a clearing in an oak wood. Steep, jagged mountains of

132

ice or glass rose beyond the wood, flashing in the sunshine. A dinosaur-like dragon capered out of the oak wood, breathing fire. A knight rode out of the castle over the drawbridge, levelling his lance. Up on the topmost tower stood a lady; wired veils of gauze wafted from her high steeple hat.

"Fairyland!" exclaimed Weinberger. "All the facets of fairyland . . .!"

He thrust the doors shut before they could witness the outcome of the dragon-tilt, and pulled them wide once more.

A great cavern with an underground river rushing through it . . . Bones littered the stone floor. A wicker cage penned a weeping, hand-wringing maiden. A giant, with nail-studded club over one shoulder, grabbed for them. Its fist slammed into the doors as both men threw their weight against them. They forced the twin doors shut against increasing pressure, till they clicked home. Then there was no more resistance from beyond.

Plucking at Jim's sleeve, Weinberger urged him along to the next alcove and the next set of doors.

Weinberger opened these more cautiously.

A white rabbit wearing a frock coat ran past, feverishly consulting a pocket watch . . .

Again: a bilious, lime-green, goggle-eyed toad rowed lazily along a winding river under the feathery drip of willow trees. The toad sported a straw boater with a candy-striped hatband, a loud checkered jacket and a mustard-yellow waistcoat. The toad was puffing on a fat cigar . . .

On they went to the next alcove.

Here the doors opened on to some future city, or some city on another world. The two men stood high on a railed tower, looking down. Gossamer bridges spanned rose-red canyons. Craft flew through the air, flapping metal wings like birds. The sun in the sky was hugely swollen, a dying bonfire red. When they reopened this same door a moment later, bloated glassy spiders the size of houses floated through a violet sky above a tawny desert, their dangling webs snaring angular white birds . . .

"They're *genre* doors, that's what," said Weinberger. "Sets of fictions. Imaginings. Free creations. Not hells or purgatories, but *inventions*. Folk invention, personal invention."

But beyond the next double doors lay a perfectly normal town suburb of white clapboard houses with green-tiled pitched roofs, neat lawns and hedges. A parade was in progress, with drum majorettes and a pipe band . . .

"Perhaps this is a memory of the ordinary — the humdrum?"

"Yes." Jim smiled. "I can hear the humdrum playing."

"It's somewhere to go back to at night, after fighting dragons and rescuing maidens?"

"They're probably all busy swopping wives and husbands there, and holding black masses."

"You just hold a black mass here, boy, and you'll get what you summon!"

"So maybe this is Horrorville, or Sexville?"

What lay beyond the next doors was quite incomprehensible, unless it was an example of abstract invention. Differently coloured lights hummed about a great three-dimensional abacus. Musical tones sounded in a constantly varying warble . . .

"If we go through one of these doorways, can we get back again from the other side?"

"No idea, Nathan. Maybe. Probably. But we aren't here for the scenery!"

All this while, they had been moving closer to the final doorway where Death hung. Now they quickened their pace towards it. From the gilded carving above those doors, Death squeaked at them plaintively.

"It wants in," said Weinberger. "Who usually opens the door for it?"

Wary of the creature hanging above his head, Jim reached for the handles, which were shaped like rams' horns. Pulling both doors wide open, he stepped back. Immediately Death flitted through the doorway, down the wide short corridor beyond.

After about thirty feet this corridor opened directly on to a pearly space. In the midst of the space floated what looked like a child's drawing of a treetop on fire with little flames, or a burning bush uprooted. As they watched, some 'leaves' zipped away like red meteor streaks. Others arrowed in from outside the pearly space. They were neither leaves nor flames. They were the Death creatures, roosting in their aviary: hundreds, perhaps thousands of them. Every moment a few left; every moment a few returned.

Half-way down the corridor stood a gold-lacquered bamboo

screen that reminded Jim of the pipes of a choir organ. From behind this screen stepped a tall red angel.

This was no human angel, though. It was no man or woman with white wings.

The angel stood over six feet tall. Its body and limbs were thin and rigid, like a stick insect's. The wings sprouting from its back were those of a death's-head hawkmoth. Its head was disproportionately large, with big faceted eyes. It had a prim little mouth, of cartilage. It was a thing of great strength — and lightness. And it was as red as Death.

"Don't worry," it said, watching them a thousand times over with its eyes. Its voice was chirrupy.

"How you see me is not *exactly* how we are. I could have appeared to you as a copy of a man, but that would have been misleading. Better by far that you meet me as an alien creature. This will assist your understanding of the situation."

"What situation?" asked Jim. "What are you?" He knew, as he spoke, that this was merely an automatic, parrot response. So long as the being did not move towards them, they were safe. Provisionally.

In the pearly space outside, the red mites of Death roosted upon that free-floating network of branching spars. Constantly, as if at a hidden signal, one or two streaked away; others streaked back . . . So the angel, then, was their Master: the true Master of the House of Death. One of their Masters, at any rate.

"Could we possibly sit down?" asked Weinberger, in more practical vein. He gestured at the Death-infested space. "Somewhere away from *that*?"

"Oh yes. If you will return to the Long Hall which you have shaped, I will follow you. At a polite distance."

"Are you real?" demanded Jim, not wanting to turn his back on the being.

The angel twitched its wings, perhaps impatiently, perhaps in amusement.

"That is a large question to discuss in a corridor, when your friend is dying to sit down."

Was 'dying to sit down' a joke? If this angel could make jokes, perhaps it could be trusted. But if it was the Master of Death, which imprisoned souls . . .?

"If you want me to make any sense to you," added the angel, "you must tell me your story first. You must tell me exactly how you came here — why and wherefore."

"Have we got time for that?"

"Time? He asks me if he has time! You don't know what time is, or untime either. Or space and unspace, for that matter. Did you come all this way — I ask you seriously — just to return immediately, with your eyes still seeing only what they expect to see?"

"Okay, *sorry*, we'll go and sit down."

Jim followed Weinberger back into the long hall. The angel followed Jim.

While the two men settled themselves into one of the brocaded sofas, the angel strode over to the wall and began to tap here and there as though to test its solidity. Finding one section which returned a hollow echo, it twisted a boss. A panel fell open on hidden hinges. The compartment inside held a quart bottle of whisky, three glasses and an ice bucket.

"Name your poison," said the angel.

"Neat," said Weinberger. The angel poured a couple of fingers of whisky. Reaching out with exaggerated discretion till it almost overbalanced, it passed the glass to Weinberger.

"That's the whisky you wanted back in the shack," whispered Jim. Weinberger swallowed half of the drink then nursed the rest.

"What if it is?"

"Then it isn't *real*."

"It tastes real enough to me."

"Neat, or on the rocks?" the angel asked Jim. "It is curious how those who worry about wasting time proceed to waste it. *Obviously* this is a place that *you* have shaped. Somewhere that *you* have defined. However, I share it with you. That is its nature: it can be shared."

"Neat," said Jim. "Please."

The angel poured, and passed the glass, stretching out again in a parody of delicacy.

"What a waste of ice," it remarked. "Someone must have wanted ice. Me, perhaps?" The angel popped a cube into its mouth and crunched the ice up. Then it poured itself some whisky.

So angels drank whisky with the dead, did they?

Its wings fluttered briefly.

"Interesting taste — like drinking brown electricity."

"Is that what you usually drink? Electricity?"

"Electricity belongs to space, my dear, not to unspace. Let us exchange names, shall we? It will make everything so much easier, since you people are beset by names for everything."

Which was something that Ananda had told Jim . . .

"I'm Jim," said Jim.

"Nathan," said Nathan.

"You may call me Tulip."

"That's a ridiculous name!" protested Jim. "You don't look remotely like a tulip."

"All the better to call me by! Our true names are the signatures of our being. A word cannot serve that purpose. But perhaps you're right . . . What name do you think best suits me?"

"Death's-head Hawkmoth."

"Too much of a mouthful — like that ice. How about . . .?"

"Al," suggested Weinberger. "Al the Alien."

"How about . . . Lal? Why not? Yes, Lal it is. Now, will you tell me exactly how you came here, and why, and what conclusions you draw?"

"You invented the cage, Nathan. You tell him."

And this Weinberger proceeded to do, while Lal remained standing with its whisky glass clasped in one claw-like extremity, its other arm resting on the drinks shelf. Occasionally, as it listened, it freshened its own glass.

TWENTY-FIVE

WHEN WEINBERGER WAS done, Lal divided what little remained of the whisky between their three glasses. This time the angel did not bother to keep its distance. It sat down on the end of the sofa, draping a thin arm around Weinberger's shoulder. To his credit, Weinberger did not flinch.

'This angel's drunk,' thought Jim. 'What a situation: we've imagined ourselves a drunken alien angel.'

"Now then," said Lal, "you've got everything inside-out and backside foremost, of course. But to your credit, you did imagine a way to come here, and imagine a 'here' to come to. This makes us rejoice.''

With its free hand, Lal toasted them.

"Cheers, beings of ordinary life, who are still alive! So you think of the red creatures as parasites that prey upon dying consciousness? You think that they haul dying souls off into the crystal fog to fertilise those crystals? Now *why* would they do that, I wonder? What's in it for them? Eh, Nathan?''

"They feed off the emotions of the trapped souls. They eat the phoney events. That's their nectar. That's their entertainment.''

"Then who am I? I must be the ringmaster! Perhaps it is we angels who feed and amuse ourselves, while they are only the messenger boys and go-betweens — the pimps of the crystal brothel? The creatures, by the way, *are* our own artificial children. I might as well admit that right away. Oh yes, we direct them.

"As you guessed, if a human being dies very suddenly our messengers don't get there in time — swift as they are! They don't home in on the pheromone of death, which you — alone of all your kind — have correctly identified as the psychochemical of dying. It does indeed alert other living creatures to an impending death. But it plays a far more important role for the dying person himself! It weans the dying spirit away from the shadows of the ordinary world. It counteracts the attractions of the ordinary and familiar. The pheromone *disintoxicates* the soul — otherwise it might simply linger on as an earth-bound ghost.''

"There must be a hell of a lot of ghosts haunting Russia and China,'' said Weinberger. "Still intoxicated.''

Lal wagged an admonishing finger.

"Obviously everyone who dies suddenly doesn't automatically become a ghost — or your world would have been packed out with ghosts long ago. Only a very small number of sudden fatalities actually meet that fate. You see, the pheromone is an evolutionary vestige from the time when your souls were less *coherent* than they are now. Many spirits passed into the earth and trees and rocks back in earlier times. There is the source of your earth-spirits, your earth magic, your Japanese *kami*. Etcetera. The pheromone was an evolutionary development when your souls were relatively weaker than they are now.

"Anyhow, let us suppose that our little friends don't get there in time. What happens then?"

"It would be better to dissolve into limbo," said Jim, "than to carry on indefinitely in some hell or purgatory."

"Oh, such lack of imagination! No wonder you could only come up with a rather large hallway, in quite atrocious taste, for this encounter of ours. And earlier, you shaped a world which wouldn't even solidify properly. Though *that*, admittedly, was because you were still alive. No doubt its failure to solidify saved you from its clutches."

Emptying its glass, Lal set it down noisily on the parquet floor.

"And I wish there was some more of this whisky. Really, your sense of provisioning is too poor — as witness your bold hike into the wilderness! Oh don't worry, I am only speaking flippantly. Really, I enjoy our conversation. It's quite unique. How I shall sing about it, how I shall dance it in unspace! Tush, do you think that I speak as an impresario again? As an artist of a higher plane, who sculpts with souls? I suppose it's just as well there isn't any more whisky . . .

"Now where — yes, *where* — do you imagine that all those suddenly dead souls go, if our own little Deaths don't grab them and snip the umbilical cord and haul them off protesting? As I said, your souls are relatively stronger nowadays. Relatively."

"If they don't become ghosts," answered Jim, "and you say that the vast majority don't, obviously they must go into the crystal fog."

"And they don't get through it, mister. They don't make it. Very few even have the wisdom or the insight to try. But those who do are doomed to failure because of the sheer extent of the fog these days.

"I use the word 'days' loosely, of course! Time is a little different here, you realize? Days and hours belong to the realm of suns and worlds, and all the other clocks of ordinary space. You actually came here in mere moments, though as to the time you spend here . . ."

"We couldn't have spent more than an *hour* in that crystal we blundered into, but when we got back —"

"Don't blame me for your blunders! Ah, but I am being short-tempered . . . Blame it on the booze." The angel rubbed its forehead.

"Are you telling us that all those little Deaths are hauling people *clear through* the fog — which would trap them otherwise? The fog hasn't got anything to do with you? It's just something in the way — an enemy?"

"Eggs-actly, Jim. We are your bosom buddies, did you but know it. Of course it's better that you don't know it. If you did, you'd be queueing all the way from birth to euthanasia to avoid dying suddenly. You characters do everything to excess on that little world of yours. You would abolish your species. Far better that some are lost than that there are no more new folk ever again."

"We already came pretty close to abolishing our species."

"In the late, great atom-splitting war? Indeed. Oh, there was a terrible boost to the opposition because of that damnfool war. The fog grew so much greater all of a sudden. You'd already killed enough people in all your recent wars to cause us grave concern, but this was the bloody limit. And then our little Deaths couldn't even keep up with all those who died slowly in the aftermath, even though they rushed to and fro, working overtime. The number of our little Deaths is based on average death statistics, you see — like one of your old insurance companies, *hic*?"

Lal hiccuped. The angel's words were still fluent enough, but it seemed to Jim that Lal was by now definitely supporting itself upon Weinberger's shoulder. Obviously whisky affected an alien angel powerfully; and Lal had drunk the lion's share of it. Would they find out the truth before Lal succumbed to its effects? Or was that the whole point: they couldn't find out?

Lal's hand patted Weinberger rhythmically a few times, like a metronome.

"Ah, but your society of Good Death is a fine thing! Yes, we influenced it. We can't make direct contact with you living people, except in such rare circumstances as these now, my buddies. But we influenced it imag-in-atively — though the shock which opened your imaginations to us was your own doing. I refer to the war."

"Don't tell me that you're responsible for Norman Harper's output!" cried Weinberger. "Don't tell me you're his muse!"

"A very hidden muse . . . Otherwise we would sabotage our own plan, you see? If people knew that there *was* a state beyond death, and that the alternative was to be encysted like a fly in amber by the crystal fog, well, you might easily euthanase yourselves away, eh?

140

Our little Deaths could never cope with the demand. It would become a runaway thing, a hysteria. You must be a very hysterical lot or you wouldn't fight wars. Stands to reason."

"Norman Harper." Weinberger groaned. "That . . . that twiddler of words."

"Don't blame *us* for your low aesthetic standards," said Lal, aggrieved. "Harper's popular, isn't he? By and large, I'm sorry to say, your imaginations are fairly meagre. Though acceptable, acceptable . . . I guess that comes from living a world-bound 'life'. So don't blame yourselves. You do improve with keeping — once you can grasp the possibilities. 'Mind-wings *can* fly.' Personally I would blame your deficient imaginations on the way that commerce polluted your art for so long. You packaged the products of your imagination like cans of peaches with pretty labels on them, and lots of syrup inside. We, on the other hand, who inhabit a wholly imaginative realm . . . But I should not boast in my cups." Lal's foot twitched, accidentally knocking over the empty whisky glass. The angel glanced down. "You do make some fairly decent liquor . . . I think I'm going to sleep."

"Don't!" cried Jim.

The angel's red eyes looked distinctly bloodshot.

"To think I shot Harper," muttered Weinberger. "And now he's stuck in some damn crystal."

"Some crystal Parnassus, perhaps?" Lal patted the man consolingly. "So you see, my buddies, your quest is an utterly mistaken one. You should surrender, and die gently. Then you can come back here the usual way, shepherded by our little Deaths, and get on with the real business."

"And what," asked Jim, "might that be?"

"Tell me, Jim old buddy, how did unspace seem to you? By unspace I mean the zone you were in just before this rather empty vestibule took its place."

"It was like an infinite number of possible places — worlds, rooms, I dunno — which all coexisted with each other. You could choose one. You could enter any one that you —"

"Could imagine." Lal cut him off. The alien waved its free hand around. "Since this is a sharing place, you can't help but see doorways to other possibilities. But you've put all those possibilities behind closed doors, haven't you? The picture frames should be

141

your catalogue — your screen, your window — but they're all blank. Unspace, Jim, is the realm of the infinite sharing imagination where you envision worlds and domains as an act of creative genius. It is where you will never be alone, since all have access to each other. It is where you give whole worlds to others, for adventure and enlightenment and joy, and even for terror — which is a kind of fearful joy — and others in turn give these to you. It is the ultimate place of free creative energy, common to all beings. You would soon learn to open all those doors in full awareness, till you had no need of doors at all — though you might like to keep them on as a useful convention. Like a rhyme scheme.''

''What are those pesky crystals, then?''

Lal blinked at him, as though it was a very naive question.

''I believe that evolution in your own little pocket of existence gave rise to the predator and prey relationship? It generally does! How else could anything evolve to any great extent, other than by competition? Why should you think it's any different after your worldly death? It's just the same, old son. But now the stakes are larger than life. Much larger. A prey who gets caught is stuck in what you folks call Hell.''

''The crystal fog is Hell?''

''A living Hell. In the sense that anything is 'living' here, it is alive. Which is another way of saying that it is deadly purposeful — as are we all. As you noticed, unspace is made up of infinitely many parts, which all arise out of each other and coexist. The fog is a native inhabitant of unspace. It evolved here. But it is the ultimate in *separation*. Once a part of it has successfully encysted itself around you, it *has you*, boy. You never reach the sharing possibilities of unspace. And oh, is there a pile-up of the fog around your world! Was it breeding fast, till we took a hand! Really, it was seriously unbalancing the whole ecology of unspace. Which is why we bred our aviary of little Deaths from out of our own selves, as a rescue operation. Certainly we are altruistic and generous — since unspace is a place of sharing — but we must confess to a certain self-interest too. The pile-up was getting oppressive. It spread too far.''

''Generous?'' echoed Weinberger. ''One of your little Deaths cured me. I was sick, and it burnt me clean. I guess that's generosity, all right.''

Lal undraped its arm from Weinberger and stood up, on the second attempt, rocking about a bit. The angel flapped its wings to steady itself, then it half-walked, half-flew to the door. Putting two claw digits to its mouth, it whistled shrilly.

TWENTY-SIX

RED DEATH STREAKED through the doorway. Braking in mid-air, it alighted hawklike on Lal's thin wrist.

Lal whistled several more times, and other little Deaths sped through the door. They circled the hall, and hung themselves on carved headpieces and empty picture frames.

"If you want my opinion," said Lal, "Death was just trying to get away from you. You being alive, and all. But you entangled it imag-in-atively, in your own death-knot. Poor simple thing, it had to unravel that knot before it could escape. And it did. What did you want to do with the little Death: exhibit it in a zoo? What a wild scheme: to cage Death, when it is itself the pass-key!"

Jim had been watching the newly-arrived Deaths nervously.

"Lal, you said that unspace is a place —"

"It is all places that you can possibly imagine yourself entering."

"You said that it's a *sharing* place — but it's full of fierce competition, too. How can it be both?"

"Competitive sharing: isn't that the very definition of a living ecology? The same holds true of the ecology of death. But I think I see your point. You worry about cruelty and oppression — about the misuse of one being by another. Let me assure you, *that* doesn't happen here. We compete in the *desirability* of our world creations: their attractiveness, their inventiveness. The finer they are, the more they will be common to all. The more everyone will wish to share them and enjoy them, and be fulfilled by them, and maybe even suffer in them. But the crystal fog knows nothing of this. It's like a virus, which only wants to repeat itself. The fog would crystallize unspace into separate cells which have no connection with each other. It would freeze the imagination into endlessly repeating patterns — of self-worlds."

Lal hoisted Death aloft.

143

"This one will guide you home. The others will escort you. Hurry now! I suspect that your time is up."

"You said that time didn't matter!"

"What do you want, a guided tour of infinity? You must gain that by your own efforts. As to time, why, time flexes in and out. Sometimes a moment is a million years, sometimes an afternoon is a moment. Now I have business, dear drinking buddies, and the cup is empty. I wish you well. Go gently, as the poet says. And since no one will believe you back home, don't bother trying to tell them, eh? Just, go gently. Then you'll soon be back, by the front door."

Tossing Death into the air, Lal skipped off on tiptoes, fluttering its wings. Becoming airborne, the being glided ineptly through the doorway, banging one wing against the jamb. Jim thought he heard it swear before it disappeared.

"So long, angel," Weinberger called after it. "Nice meeting you."

Death buzzed them. It darted ahead, it returned coaxingly. The other Deaths took wing and dived to catch at the men's clothes and hair, pulling them.

"And here's the bum's rush, out of infinity. Okay, okay, we're going."

The two men began walking, then trotting, then running, nagged by Deaths which were pestering them like starlings mobbing a couple of owls. The faster they ran, the further away the other end of the hall seemed to become, the vaster the floor space, the higher the domed ceiling. Either the room was swelling to enormous proportions, or else they were shrinking. The two men were so tiny now that they had lost all weight and were flying along above the floor.

What floor? What walls? Space extended around them indefinitely: space of a pearly hue. Far ahead bulged a wall of white fog . . . The Deaths had ceased their harrying tactics by now and were flying wing in a V-formation like migrating ducks, with the little Death-guide at the forward point. The void was smoothly empty. Soon the wall of fog ahead began to resolve itself into innumerable jostling coloured specks . . .

Jim sat up, with a groan. He felt as though he had been dragged through a briar patch by the hair.

Weinberger also opened his eyes. Immediately he pointed a finger at the roof.

"It's keeping watch."

"I don't see anything . . . Oh. Wait." Something red flickered vaguely up there, almost beyond vision. Jim shook his head. He couldn't see it any longer.

"It's there."

"Maybe."

"If you let it be there, it's there."

"Our guardian angel?"

"No, Lal was the angel. That thing's just a self-propelled feather from Lal's wings. Knotted up into a creature. I think there are two of them up there."

Whatever Lal had said about time flexing in and out, by now it was late afternoon. The batteries of the cassette player had run down. The rain had quit lashing the lake. Earth and sky had unmixed. Once again, clouds definitely belonged in the sky; and as the clouds drifted by, they broke apart so that ragged patches of sunlight ran across the dull waters outside like searchlight beams hunting for the shack. But with no interest in finding it, only in picking out arbitrary stencil shapes.

Jim stared up at the place where the little Deaths either lurked, or did not lurk. Really, he couldn't be sure — and staring hardly helped him see them. Obviously the corner of Weinberger's eye was more acute than Jim's.

"Do you know something, Nathan? I believe we've run out of reasons for escaping."

"Because we've been where we wanted to go?"

Jim nodded. "And what could we tell our 'friends' over the border now? 'Hey, if you get squashed by a train or electrocuted, you'll go to Hell! Play it safe, and you'll reach the free spaces. Play it dangerous, and that's that, baby.' That's no philosophy for a world."

"You have a point, old drinking buddy. Where would people get the spunk to create anything half-way imaginative after they were dead? Lal forgot to mention *that*."

"Right. He was just worried in case we all killed ourselves quickly and quietly. Which is precisely what *we* ought to arrange for ourselves!"

145

"What?"

"I don't mean right now. I don't mean we should shoot ourselves. I guess the adrenalin begins pumping when you're faced by a gun. Fight-or-flight sets in, and the death pheromone hasn't got a look in. No, we should get back to Egremont — back to the House. We'll apply for immediate euthanasia, you and I. Don't you see the logic of it, knowing what we do? I'll take this straight to Menotti. He can't refuse an Application Absolute, backed by both client and guide. And I certify you well and truly guided, Nathan." Jim grinned crookedly. "Me too. At least fifty miles well guided . . . which is a bit of a nuisance."

"What about Resnick?"

"Ah yes, your public appearance . . . Sally Costello must have told Menotti about that scheme, even if Resnick didn't. I think I can put it to Menotti that Resnick is simply serving his own ego — and what's more, that it would actually do horrible harm to the House and all the other Houses to set you up on your hind legs on a platform. Some of the things you'd say would really blow the roof off everything! What things? Well, we aren't telling. Leave 'em puzzled. Leave Resnick bewildered. Serve him right."

"He might put the cage together again, just to find out?"

"Alice Huron would never let him. Besides, you control the world supply of the pheromone."

Weinberger lifted the dispenser flask, still dangling from the fishing line.

"Not any more. Nobody does. It's all gone." He licked his lips. "Like they say, I'll take the secret with me to the grave."

"You agree, then?"

"I guess so. I could hardly suspect you of some cunning scheme to guide me all the way through the countryside back to my own deathbed."

"Oh, Nathan."

"Just joking, old buddy. I realize that you're heading for your deathbed too. Shall we make a start? It'll take us two or three days."

"It won't, if they're still flying around looking for us. Waving a red flag from a treetop mightn't do much good, but I bet you that a nice smokey fire will attract some attention! It's a bit closed in here for that — we ought to be on higher ground. They won't bother

146

parachuting the troops in if we're jumping up and down beside a bonfire, waving to them. They'll send a helicopter. We'll ride back in style. Let's eat, then we can decide about starting back.''

"I need sugar. I want something sweet."

Jim dug into his valise and produced a large can of peach slices with a bright, sunny label.

Weinberger swilled the last of the syrup out of the can, and set it down neatly.

"There's one thing we never found out. Aren't Lal and his crew aiming to do anything *tough* about the crystal fog? Can't they smash it up or something? We should have asked. But we got the bum's rush.''

Jim considered.

"It sounded to me more as though they were just keeping it in check — ecologically. Maybe the crystal cells crack up after a few million subjective years? So people do get out again. Maybe the whole thing reaches a population climax and dies down? I have a sneaking suspicion that the fog's no worse for Lal and company than a patch of weeds in the back of the flower border is for us. They hold their garden parties on the lawn. True, the weeds can spread like wildfire . . .''

"Lal was a *nicer* fellow than that.''

"But if the crystals are natives of that region, how do they come to be there in the first place? Ecologically speaking? Prey and predator relationship, oh sure — but maybe the fog preys *particularly* on sick souls, unhealthy souls, ones that aren't mature enough? Like an antibody or phagocyte. Perhaps it keeps unspace clean by catching those souls and binding on to them and purging them in purgatories? Lately, it's gotten out of hand — and it's all our fault.''

"How?''

Jim sucked his fingers then wiped them dry on his trousers.

"Once, if you were half-way wise you could get through the fog. Or simply because the fog was thinner, you could. But all of a sudden we overpopulated the world, then we killed a billion people in a flash. They all got in each other's way. The fog soaked them up, dividing and redividing like nuclear fission. Now it's so dense that it traps everyone whom the little Deaths can't reach in time.

147

It's going to take us a long time to know all the answers to the ecology of unspace.''

"The angels know them. The dead aliens."

"And we're just juniors. Not graduates of Death."

"Not yet!"

"The Earth is our kindergarten. That's why Lal doesn't want us all to kill ourselves."

"But *we* will," grinned Weinberger.

"Right. Client and guide no longer — but partners in dying."

Outside of the glassless window the sky had half cleared and the clouds which remained were being stained by a fine sunset. With luck, this might be the last earthly sunset they ever saw. They had seen enough sunsets in their lives, Jim thought, to imagine many finer ones hereafter.

Jim made up his mind.

"We'll stay here tonight. The ground'll be damp outside. There's no sense in catching our death of cold."

"I told you, you don't catch cold —!"

Jim grinned raffishly. "Nor do you catch Death. Death catches us. We hope."

"I don't feel sleepy."

"You never do. But you might as well enjoy the experience while it lasts."

"Yeah, I wonder whether the dead sleep? I hope they don't. Though Lal said he felt sleepy when the booze hit him."

"One thing the dead certainly do is *dream*. Wide awake. And they share their dreams around."

TWENTY-SEVEN

THEY CAME UPON a forest road around mid-morning. Though they were heading southwards again, they found it impossible to retrace the exact route by which they had come. The rain — or simply the act of turning around to face in the opposite direction — seemed to have washed out the half-remembered landmarks of the earlier journey. They had wandered to the east.

They followed the rough road steadily uphill through trees for the best part of an hour, till they saw the top of a firetower rising above the pines.

"Just the job!" Jim rubbed his hands together, as though to start a fire in them.

The firetower stood in half an acre of cleared ground; it was a high wooden pylon with a cabin perched on top. Windows looked out over the forest in all four directions, and a roofed verandah ran around, open to the wind. Overhead, the thin whip of an aerial ticked back and forth. Access was by way of a rung ladder up the inside of the pylon, to a trap door in the bottom of the cabin.

They climbed up.

The cabin was deserted. Its battery radio had been removed, along with any fire-spotting equipment. But there were bunks and a table and two chairs, and a steel waste bucket.

"They only man these at high risk times," said Weinberger. "Early summer, midsummer. It's too late in the season now."

A cupboard yielded a paraffin lamp containing some fuel, an open packet of rye crispbread which tasted like straw by now, and half a dozen well-thumbed erotic paperbacks.

Stepping out on to the verandah, Jim walked about appreciating the view, storing it in his memory as raw material for worlds as yet uninvented. Despite intrusive crags and peaks it was not utterly unlike the view in Weinberger's scene-screen back at the House. Southward lay Egremont, Lake Tulane and all the deciduous trees of the valley flanks which would spread a rug of red and gold against the green . . . but they were too far away.

They carried the two chairs out on to the verandah, placing them at the south-east corner where they could talk to each other while scanning half the sky. Jim brought out the waste bucket, the reservoir base of the lamp, and all the paperbacks.

Back inside, he upended his valise on the table, tipping everything out. He dropped the empty bag through the trapdoor and followed it, down the ladder.

By the time he got back to the verandah, lugging a bag stuffed with grass and sticks and broken branches, Weinberger was already well engrossed in one of the novels, chuckling to himself.

"Here's one fire they weren't aiming to put out!"

"Hey, you're supposed to be watching the sky."

"Good peripheral vision, Jim: that's what got me into this — I guess it can get me out of it, too."

149

Sacrificing the least appealing of the paperbacks, page by scrumpled page, Jim half filled the bucket and tamped the paper down with sticks and straw. Then, tilting back his chair and planting his feet on the rail, he too settled himself to read a novel. He kept one eye on the horizon. The book he had picked up was entitled *House of Lust*. It was unlike any work he had scanned before, but he had to admit that it had its passing attractions. Though was it quite the proper reading matter before he launched himself into the afterlife?

He had just reached chapter four when Weinberger said, "Hey!"

Jim followed his finger. There in the south was the white speck of a monoplane. Presently a faint droning reached their ears.

"Not yet . . . Ah, go to it!"

Jim poured the paraffin into the bucket and dropped in a lighted match. He fed in wads of grass and pine cones; smoke billowed up around the verandah. He dropped the novels in one by one, then relieved Weinberger of his reading matter and pitched that in too. It was a brief fire but a dirty one.

"Here it comes!"

The two men leaned out, waving.

The white Peace Service monoplane circled the firetower twice, then waggled its wings and headed back towards the south.

They settled down to wait.

"Nothing to read now," grumbled Weinberger. "Just as it was getting interesting, too!"

An hour later they heard a thin chattering whirr. Again, Weinberger was the first to spot the flying speck.

"Chopper! You were right, Jim."

The helicopter sped across the forest towards the tower, trimming the trees like an upside-down lawn mower. If it hit a treetop, thought Jim, and crashed in a ball of flames then its riders would end up trapped in the crystal fog through no fault of their own . . .

The helicopter neared, slowed and hovered. The two men waved.

Something — a tube — poked out of an open perspex window. A sharp crack sounded. Immediately splinters of wood flew from the verandah rail. A few of these splinters stabbed Jim's left hand.

As both men dived for the cabin door, the south-facing window shattered.

Inside, they crouched.

"Those were bullets, Jim!"

"I didn't think they were dried peas."

"They're trying to kill us — by surprise! If they do that . . . we'll never find our way through the fog. We'll be encysted."

Weinberger stared up at the roof in anguish.

"My little Death," he cried, "where are you? We need you now!"

But there was nothing up there.

"Shit, why are they shooting? Bullets! Violence! How can it happen?"

"You're a fine one to talk."

"There was a reason for shooting Harper — even if it was the wrong reason. How can they shoot us down like vermin? What's *their* reason?"

"Revenge."

"*Official* revenge?"

Jim puzzled at the splinters in his hand, but they were too impacted to pull out. How could there be such a thing as official revenge? That puzzled him too.

A shot hit the roof.

"What lousy shooting! Where do they think we are? Hanging on the ceiling?"

Pulling the gun from his pocket, Jim remembered to slip off the safety catch.

"I'll scare them."

"Wait: you ought to hold that in both hands to steady it. Like this." As Weinberger mimed, he seemed to be praying. To the little Deaths, which had deserted them.

"When you shot Harper, you didn't —"

"He was closer."

"Have we any right to send our own worst enemy —?"

"They aren't worrying."

Jim stuck his head around the window frame. The helicopter hovered side-on about fifty feet away, rocking slightly.

Jim saw who held the rifle: a rifle equipped with sights.

It was Noel Resnick.

151

The helicopter pilot was Toni Bekker.

Briefly, Jim and Resnick stared at each other, recognizing each other perfectly well. Resnick ducked his head, to sight the rifle. One eye closed in what seemed to be a broad wink.

Jumping in front of the window, holding the gun in both hands, Jim fired once, twice — at the man, not the machine.

Resnick fired too.

Both men missed. Jim even missed the helicopter entirely. It was a duel of incompetents.

Bekker pulled the helicopter back another fifty feet. Another rifle slug hit the cabin inaccurately.

"That's Resnick with the rifle," said Jim, taking shelter again. "The pilot is the very same man from the Octagon who gave me this damn gun. He's *Resnick's* man."

"Resnick?" Weinberger shouted the name as though the breeze would hear and pass his protest on, whereupon Resnick would realize that he was misbehaving. "Isn't he forfeiting all right to be a Master?"

"Isn't Bekker disqualifying himself as a Peace Officer? I see it all now! Alice Huron sent them out. 'Don't come back without a scalp, Noel, or I'll withdraw your privileges. The chalet, Mary-Ann, the lot. I'll break you.' That's it. They're going to say *we* fired on them. They're going to make out that we were only pretending to give up peacefully. But actually we wanted to lure them here so that we could shoot them down!"

Jim jumped up and pumped another bullet through the broken window. It flew wild.

"Save your shots, man."

" 'This is the final test, Noel darling, to see if you can become a Controller like me! Will you commit an utter crime, to bind you to our ranks?' It's an initiation test."

"What on earth are you talking about?"

"The real, secret Controllers. I never told you about those."

"Too late now, Jim. *Save your shots.* We need some covering fire while we get out of here. That's what they used to call it: covering fire. You listen to me: the whole of the Egremont House can't possibly be in on this — nor the whole Octagon, either! We have to give ourselves up to ordinary officers. We've got to get out of here and reach Egremont on foot."

152

Another slug hit the cabin.

"We'll shin down the ladder. We'll run for the trees."

A bullet whined overhead, completely missing the cabin. Resnick must be jerking the rifle every time he pulled the trigger.

"We'll be okay. He'll miss us. People have to overcome a mighty aversion to using guns on other people. It screws up their shooting."

"It didn't screw yours up." Jim did not offer to hand the gun over to Weinberger, though. Nor did Weinberger seem anxious to be holding it.

"I'm going first, Jim. You've got three shots to fire at the chopper while you follow me. Don't worry too much about hitting it!"

"Hey —"

But Weinberger had already yanked the trapdoor open, and was scrambling down the ladder.

Nathan jumped the last half dozen feet to the ground. But he misjudged the distance. The impact twisted his ankle and he fell, the ankle a sudden ball of pain. Seizing his ankle, he squeezed it and rubbed — and heard another rifle shot whine high overhead. The worst of the pain went away quite quickly. Nothing was broken. Nathan hauled himself to his feet. His ankle was tender but he knew that he could run — limpingly.

Thirty feet above his head, Todhunter seemed to have snagged his jacket on a nail — or was it between two spars? The man looked too big and ungainly to climb down properly. Wrenching his coat free, Todhunter loosed another wild shot.

"The plane was the net!" screamed Nathan. "But Resnick is the harpoon!"

Nathan began hobble-running across the grass. Where was the helicopter, damn it? As he looked, the machine soared right over the tower, and a little bundle was tossed out.

Nathan had a couple of moments to guess what it might be, and to throw himself down with his eyes shut, before the dynamite exploded.

Nathan recovered enough senses to know that he was dying. Something had impaled him. It was frightfully painful, but somehow it was stopping his life from leaking out of him all at once.

He concentrated. The important thing was: was he dying too quickly, or not quickly enough? Would he have time for his body to realize that it was dying and begin sweating to signal Death? He hoped so. On the other hand, if Resnick got to him too soon he dreaded the prospect of a sudden *coup de grâce*. He fought the pain, so that he could fear the *coup de grâce*.

Awkwardly he turned his head. The helicopter was settling down on to grass littered with wreckage. He couldn't hear its rotors; he was deaf. The firetower no longer towered overhead, though some tall timbers stayed drunkenly erect. The tower and its cabin had been broken up and thrown around. Some piece of the pylon must be sticking through his body. Like a harpoon.

'Praise be, my little Death's here already! Ah no, it's only blood . . . spilling, spurting.'

With momentary clarity Nathan saw where Todhunter lay. For a moment he couldn't quite understand what he saw. Then he realized that Todhunter had lost his head. Permanently.

As soon as the rotor blades had stopped, Noel Resnick clambered out. The big man looked about cautiously, saw Todhunter's headless trunk, and was promptly sick upon the grass.

'Surely I've spent enough time dying by now? Surely?'

Nathan's vision blurred with a rosy haze. Was this his little Death coming flying to him now? Or was it Resnick? He summoned up a suitable insult for the man.

'Murderer.'

He wasn't sure whether he said this aloud. Actually, he thought, in most other respects Resnick — Master of the House of Death — was a *saviour* of souls.

Pain preoccupied Nathan.

TWENTY-EIGHT

JIM SWAM. Or flew. He wasn't sure which. Rapture possessed him. He had very little awareness of a body. Ahead, were . . .

Lights: great sparkling, beautiful lights! Shining facets. Coloured mirrors in which he might see who he was, and become

154

what he saw. He was tiny, and they were great — with oh so many faces, bright blank faces that yearned to picture him.

Not all of them so yearned. By no means all. Many were already 'full', he realized. They were complete. Now he felt panic. He might not find one, to complete himself.

But no; for the further through this medium he went, the more of them were available. He could sense those from afar. It was as if they scented the medium with their light, with a most compelling musky scent of light.

Yet something made him fly on further, greedily.

He was Aladdin, rushing through the cave of silver coins and the cave of gold coins — where faces were already stamped upon many of the coins — seeking for the garden with the trees of perfect jewels . . .

Memory flooded back. In horror he recalled a tiny wormlike creature with a human face being dragged willy-nilly through this very place in the beak of a red bat-moth!

The horror died, as he remembered what the bat-moth really was. Then the horror surged back again, redoubled. Nothing whatever was dragging *him* along — for his own salvation!

He knew exactly where he was. And he knew that he had died. Most suddenly.

The crystal fog was even vaster than he remembered. Or he was much smaller. The 'gravity' of the crystals was fully apparent to him now. It was a gravity of mood rather than of mass. Those crystals which were already full repelled him emotionally — and his line of flight obeyed his emotions. Available jewels tugged from afar. For the time being the various forces of repulsion and attraction seemed to balance out, allowing him to proceed as he wished — since he had no desire to be caught. But gradually the trend was becoming attractive, pulling him more fiercely.

How he struggled to keep clear of them. How he willed himself to fly right through, without coming close to any.

He flew for hours, or for minutes. No time existed. Surely he must be nearing the outer fringes now, so strongly did the empty crystals ache for him! There were many more empty ones out here.

But where was the void beyond them? Where was the lucid emptiness? Was it up? Was it down? Was it through here?

The light appeared to be whiter in one direction, less prismatic . . .

No! He turned back.

He was losing his strength. His will was ebbing.

Now he was in a cul-de-sac, a blind channel bright with azure, rose and golden icebergs. As he turned sluggishly to escape once more, fighting against some kind of current which was pressing him the other way, the ice closed up . . .

TWENTY-NINE

As THE MONORAIL train from Gracchus sped out of the final black tunnel into the honeyed sunlight, Jim beheld the enchanted valley of Egremont . . .

He saw the hills aflame, the blue mirror of Lake Tulane, the orchards, farms and factory domes, the tiny Beadway pods, the peak of the distant House of Death.

He sat, numbed by the sight.

'I'm dead. Dead. And here is my crystal prison . . .

'I'm dead because Noel Resnick shot me. (Did he *shoot* me? I'm not sure, but he certainly killed me.)

'And I know that I'm dead. So here is a world of truth, not fantasy. Here is a perfect recording of the real world.

'How perfect is it?'

All the inhabitants of this recreated Egremont — Marta and Weinberger, Resnick and Alice Huron — would be the furniture of his own mind. They would be his own memories, incarnated. Would they still be able to act with purposes and motives of their own?

With all the strength of his will he concentrated on the passing scene, trying to shift one single item in it, to force it to change into something else.

'That tree! Let it be a fountain!'

The tree was a tree was a tree.

'I'm the Controller — oh yes, I'm that now! — but things won't obey my control . . .'

Now the train was slowing as it approached the station.

On impulse he patted his pocket, in case — somehow — the gun was still there; but his pocket was empty of any gun.

Rising, he tugged down his valise. Why had he stuck it up there on the luggage rack in the first place, when the train was empty except for himself? Out of a sense of tidiness, perhaps. He had always been worried about bumping into things.

And now he had bumped into something which would hold him for an eternity . . . Though how could that be, if ordinary minutes and hours and days applied in Egremont? He had no idea. He just felt extraordinarily lonely. Where were the doors from here into other possible worlds? Nowhere. That was the nature of this place.

'Hell,' he thought, 'is the world come round again. And I'm in Hell, which is quite simply Egremont.'

A cheerful, buxom woman stood waiting for him on the platform . . .

Of course. Who else? *But could she speak freely?* Could she change her lines? For that matter, could he?

"A wonderful day, Jim!" Marta exclaimed gaily, as they shook hands. "And an especially wonderful day for Egremont."

"Yes, Norman Harper's retiring today, isn't he?"

Jim had not said that last time. He hadn't known. But Marta was not in the least put out.

"Right! Our P and J: our Pride and Joy. The ceremony's quite soon, in fact. We'll just be in time to catch it."

"Quite an auspicious moment to arrive," said Jim cautiously. "I suppose Alice Huron is going to guide him?"

"Oh yes. Though how can any of us really guide *his* death? You know Alice, do you?"

He nodded.

"She doesn't know me, though."

Marta's eyes narrowed, puzzled.

"Then how did you know —?" She faltered. "Oh, I think I see . . ." She began to move away towards the waiting electric runabout.

He caught her by the arm.

"*What* do you see?"

"Jim — Mr Todhunter — what's the matter with you? Do you feel ill?"

He let go of her.

157

"I'm all right. Sorry."

She smiled. "It's just that I don't like to get involved in, well, any sort of intrigue. There are so many more *pleasant* things going on. This beautiful day, to begin with!"

What she saw, no doubt, was that he was a secret agent involved in some kind of House politicking, and he would like to recruit her to his side as an informant.

To put her at her ease Jim said firmly, "Oh, it's nothing like that — nothing at all! I assure you, Marta, I really do. I just heard on the grapevine that Alice Huron was going to guide Harper. That's all."

Reassured, she led him to the runabout.

As they drove along, Marta pointed out the sights of Egremont: Harper Street, the Farming Co-op, the school complex where she was a guide, the famous Mall where he could dine on the finest food around at the Three Spires restaurant . . . She had recovered her jolly composure.

'Here we go again . . .'

This time, forewarned — doubly forewarned by his initial *faux pas* with Marta! — he must bide his time and trace out all Resnick's lines of power. He must work out Resnick's exact place in the spider's web which included Alice Huron and Mary-Ann Sczepanski and Toni Bekker and which extended he knew not how far, nor with how many tangles in it. Marta's reaction to his arm-grabbing question had sounded quite spontaneous, quite free. It had almost set up an entirely different situation with regard to her, losing him perhaps her friendly trust.

'Hell is a lot more complicated to live in than I thought . . .' He felt no pain as such. Only the ache of loneliness, and the strain of the exhausting, futile mental acrobatics he would have to perform to lead a feasible 'life' here.

This time at least (he promised himself) he must certainly go to bed with someone! Someone other than Nathan Weinberger . . .

Weinberger . . .! Harper. The ceremony!

Marta and he were driving towards a *murder*, a murder which was so much a part of him by now that it seemed ordinary and obvious — a murder which he could still *prevent*.

Yet if he did prevent it, then Weinberger would inevitably remain in Mary-Ann Sczepanski's charge, and so by proxy in Resnick's clutches. Jim would never have an excuse to work with him.

"... I oughtn't to tell you, but we've fixed up a 'get-to-know-you' barbecue out at the Lake this evening."

"Sounds great," said Jim automatically.

"You don't sound very excited."

"Oh, I am. I am."

"You haven't tasted our local white wine, from the Vinehouse!"

"I look forward to it, Marta. Really I do." *But it won't happen this evening. It won't happen till Friday evening, by which time everything will have changed.*

'And I shall be working with Nathan by then — doing what?

'Why, building a cage for Death!'

Yes, the first thing he must do was build a cage for Death, to catch one of those little red go-between crittus and force it to lead him out of here. Out of this crystal prison which bound him, in a perfect retake of Egremont. Out into unspace, into freedom.

'It should take me with it right away. I'm already dead.'

But would it be a *real* Death which he caught in Weinberger's cage? Could he really summon one of those creatures into this crystal — or would he only imagine that he did so?

'Who needs to build a cage? I only need the Mike Mullen tape, and I've already got that, and the Neo-H pills from the pharmacy. And the pheromone, of course — I need that, and Weinberger has it, left in his sealed apartment under lock and key. There's no way of getting in there without authority. So I'll have to play along with Nathan's present fears. We'll just have to build the cage, after all ...'

But how could he possibly allow Harper to be murdered, this very afternoon, in perhaps half an hour or an hour? How could he let the poet be killed by surprise, so that a very deserving man (his poetry aside) went to Hell?

"... and that's the Octagon. Our Peace Office."

There was, of course, no church in Egremont. Egremont was a model of an enlightened, well-adjusted community ...

But this particular Norman Harper was only part of the furniture of Jim's own mind! As was the Weinberger who waited ahead, with the hidden gun.

Yet Marta — and presumably everyone else — appeared to be thoroughly alive. Pinch Marta and she would squeal, and Jim would suffer the consequences.

If he did pinch her, maybe the runabout would go out of control. Maybe they would crash.

At a sedate fifteen miles per hour this would hardly do much damage — but suppose they were travelling much faster? Could Jim be killed, when he was already dead? Alternatively, could he take his own life?

Would he simply find himself back on the monorail train, heading into Egremont forever and forever?

The House of Death and the Hospital rose up ahead, twin pyramids clad in gardens.

Maybe this had already all happened before not once but many times? With the difference that *this time*, uniquely, he remembered!

If that was so, then the tipsy alien angel called Lal and all the little Deaths and the whole crystal fog would be the furniture of his mind too!

Oh, how this crystal which had encysted him must be feasting on his misery and doubt! If the crystal existed at all . . .

Perhaps there had once been a 'real' world far from here, quite different from Egremont and Gracchus and the society of death? Jim tried to imagine what it might have been like.

'I was actually a priest, who lost his faith — or who never had one. A priest with an itchy, frustrated libido. And Marta and Weinberger and all the others were my parishioners, whom I utterly failed. And this is what God has done to me. But I never believed in God. There's only unspace — and the crystal fog. I never believed in God, so He isn't here. His House isn't here.

'Why was I a priest? Because I couldn't cope with the intrigues of life. Only with the simplicity of death. I must have killed myself when I still couldn't cope with the deviousness, the life politics. I tried to run out on it all into the empty wilderness, of death. So now I have to repeat over and over again what I couldn't cope with when I was alive: the web of relationships, and lust, and power . . . It all got so complicated that I felt I was going mad with the complexities that other people take for granted. Easing people out of life into death would be just the way I'd try to trim the world, wouldn't it? Dead people are simpler than living people. (Only, they bloody well aren't here!) So I simplified things. Because I didn't understand them. I didn't understand sex or money or politics. Or relationships. It was easier to be a priest, except that I didn't believe. Or I stopped believing. Or my belief was taken away from me . . .'

As they turned into the concourse between the Hospital and the House, Jim prayed.

There was no response. How could there be? This other life of his was only a passing fantasy.

'There *are* no more priests, damn it! Well, give or take a few hundred who've gone underground into priest holes, with powerful protectors. Their God was just an early morning mist. And I was never one of those! Whatever made me think it? I'm a guide, and a good one. I only failed as a guide because of the damned intrigues. But I did succeed in one thing: I found out what death really is.

'And *this* is my death: trapped inside one jewel in the crystal fog — a jewel where one man aches alone.

'And this is my *first* repeat of Egremont.

'I'm in danger of losing my sanity here. What is insanity? Complete disconnection from the world, that's what. So all the captive dead are mad.'

As Marta opened the door of the runabout, Jim felt like cudgelling his forehead with his fists. But he got out. He allowed Marta to tug him along by the arm, down through the ranks of the audience. Earlier he had grabbed her arm; now she grabbed his, in mischievous reprise. She was solid, she was wholesome. He desired her.

They sat together on the turf.

"That's Norman Harper on the left."

"Yes. Of course."

But Jim was staring at Mark Barnes, the natty negro Mayor of Egremont. Today was the only day when Jim would have a chance to see him, according to the way events went before. Where was the Mayor's place in all the chains of relationships?

"And Alice Huron. But you already know all about her." Marta nudged him slyly in the ribs.

('Nudge me again.')

"Oh, I *told* you I hadn't met her," he lied.

'Mark Barnes,' he thought. How could any relationships or connections possibly be hidden from him if they were just the furniture of his mind?

161

"And Dr Claudio Menotti — he's our euthanaser."

The reason was that so much of his own mind was hidden from itself. He remembered all the switches and mazes which he had dreamt about feverishly on that first night of sleeping rough.

'They're *all* my people. That's why I imagined for a ridiculous few moments that I might really be a priest — in pastoral charge of them. I haven't been able to get to know them properly, that's all.'

When one of these furniture-people died: was a reflection of a soul able to lose its way in a reflection of the crystal fog? Was that possible? Was Jim perhaps only a reflection — as in Weinberger's mirrors? A self-aware reflection?

'No, no, no again!'

After scanning the sky speculatively for rain clouds, the Mayor of Egremont rose to speak.

Marta was all ears, but Jim looked round. Time to locate Weinberger! Yes, there sat Nathan on the turf, two rows behind. Jim's past and future partner directed a wildly furtive glance at him as he realized that he was being scrutinised. He looked like a cat caught mauling a baby bird in a back yard. Satisfied, Jim faced front again.

And he felt consumed by a sudden absurd warmth for the whole assembly: for Marta who might or might not go to bed with him, for Weinberger who would be his partner, for tubby Claudio Menotti whom he barely knew, even for Alice Huron seated like a ramrod at the moment but soon to bow briefly in tears. And even for Noel Resnick, up on his feet now to speak — or more exactly, up on one foot at a time.

However they acted, they were all intimately part of him; and he must love them all, whatever they did. In so doing, somehow he must save them — in order to save himself.

Yet already he had no hope of saving Norman Harper from one individual in the audience . . .

Resnick sat down, to quiet applause.

And now Norman Harper was on his feet. He looked such a kindly person. 'What a shame I never got to know him. He probably doesn't think his poetry's all that hot.

'His poetry — or is it mine?'

The poet closed his eyes, and recited.

162

"The embryo bird must partly die
If its wings are to emerge, to fly.
The caterpillar dies, as well,
To become the butterfly, so swell . . ."

'I'm responsible for all my creations. Or rather, recreations . . .
However cussedly or sweetly they behave. Because I'm responsible
for myself. But am I sure of that? No, I can't be absolutely sure. I
have to take it on trust. I have to live out this imitation second life
much more cunningly, and kindly, and excellently. Till I can work
out how to free myself . . .'

"There is no Enemy, no Thief:
A dangerous, and a false belief!
Many times in life we die
So that our new mind-wings can fly . . ."

'No! The *real* Norman Harper wrote those lines, not I!
'He wrote them once; and once he recited them.
'But now is twice.'
Jim waited for the murder to take place.
And while he waited for the inevitable event, he reached out and
squeezed Marta's hand. She regarded him with wonder. Then she
smiled and squeezed his hand in turn.

"We shall be as we were before.
The day is over, perfect day . . ."

Now it was all beginning.

THIRTY

NOEL RESNICK, MASTER of the House of Life in Montegro, whis-
tled perfunctorily as he strode along the corridor towards Special
Treatment. When he felt worried he usually whistled a few notes.
Really, we ought to change that name, he thought. 'Special
Treatment', indeed! It smacked of, well, Nazi euthanasia
practices. Whereas the only death that was on offer in that room

163

was the death of a psychosis. New life, purged of madness, was what it promised.

Obviously Todhunter had been malevolently impressed by the present name. *That* might account for a lot of things. The insane were experts at skewing the whole consensus world along some wild axis at right angles to reality. One should never offer them such misleading hints as were conveyed by 'Special Treatment'.

'Oh, we should have thought of that!'

Yet Todhunter's case was unique. Because of his earlier professional connection with the House of Life he had internalised many elements of the therapy situation in his own fantasy role-playing. Now he held a mirror up to the House which was as distorting as in any funfair crazy house.

'And now it seems we can't get him out of the mirror . . .'

Yes, the name must go. How about 'Psychoscope Therapy' instead? Not really. Too frighteningly technical, with overtones of 'psychosis' . . . 'Scope Therapy'? Neat and snappy. Better still: 'Life Game Therapy'. Yes, that was it! It sounded playful and enhancing. At the next staff seminar he would recommend the title be adopted.

Why had Alice Huron asked him to meet her in the S.T. room? Resnick had only just himself heard about the emergency — if it could be called an 'emergency', when the whole point was that Todhunter *hadn't* emerged. On the phone she had sounded conspiratorial, the possessor of secret knowledge.

Resnick shook his head. No, that was the Todhunter version of Alice. The real Alice was no devious schemer.

'Mustn't get the two mixed up.'

It was all too easy to. The Todhunter therapy, with its grotesque extrapolations upon their own lives, exerted a considerable fascination. That was why Alice had pressed to meet him in the S.T. room rather than simply calling by his office; right now it was the centre of gravity of their lives.

Could the massive distortions invented by Todhunter actually influence the House staff to behave out of character, mesmerised by their fantasy roles? Resnick feared so. '*Beware.*'

He whistled a few more tuneless notes. At least he hadn't started stuttering!

Arriving, he unlocked the outer door of the S.T. room. As he stepped inside, the door swung shut behind him, automatically locking itself. He hesitated behind the inner glass door, peering through as a scheming Resnick would have done . . .

As usual, Todhunter was lying comatose on the insulated air-cushion bed attached to drips and catheters and vital signs monitors, and wired up through his skullcap to the vacuum-sealed transducer crystals of the psychoscope.

Marta Bettijohn sat with earphones on, watching the three circular holo stages whereon, in miniature, three-dimensional ghost events of apparently solid substance were enacted. Number one was Todhunter's own viewpoint on the life game — yes, *life game*, Resnick reminded himself. Number two was a detached observer viewpoint with the holographic homunculus of Todhunter always at the center. (Resnick noted the lawn outside the House of Life, crowded with visitors . . . *for a second time*. Several people were up on a platform; he knew who they would be, without looking.) Number three was the 'associations' holo, aswirl with imagery: faces were constantly projected, and buildings and nudes and razors, ruins of churches, orgies, red bat-like creatures, steaming plates of food, lounging red angels sipping whisky, giant moths, stampeding horses. Occasionally scrolls of text ran through the holo, like subtitles on a movie. Computer discs spun behind Marta, recording all three levels of the action.

Norman Harper was squatting beside his psychoscope, tapping it in a puzzled way while still keeping one grim eye on the holo scenes.

Dr Weinberger, Todhunter's therapy guide, was listening to the audio channels too, while he watched.

Pneumatic young med-tech Sally Costello was busy with the vital signs readouts. Alice hadn't yet arrived.

Resnick entered.

"Hullo, everybody. Let's have the bad news."

Norman Harper pulled a face.

"Bad news for me. I'm about to be murdered again."

"And what's the bad news about Father Todhunter?"

"As I told you on the phone, he's recycling. He's going through it all again. But this time he knows that he's going through a repeat. We can pick that up on the subvocals. And we can't pull him out."

"Maybe he needs to go through it all again, if he didn't clear himself on the initial run?"

" 'Run' is the word for it. Right off into the hills."

Weinberger had taken off his earphones by now.

"Yes, the whole thing got progressively more unstable as we expected," he said. "First the hints and innuendos, then outright hostility. Everything became a paranoid fix. That kind of world-view couldn't hold together, because it wasn't compatible with actuality. So he had to quit Montegro. I mean Egremont. Hell, which *do* I mean?"

"I gather that I blew him up with dynamite," said Resnick dolefully. "But at least he let me dismantle his crazy cage."

"Oh yes, then ran off with the heart of it! When all the suppressed violence and self-violence came to a head, Noel, he should have been cleared — purged. Just as I was, of my . . . cancer." Weinberger looked slightly sick. "*That* imagery was clear enough — in so far as it got dumped on my shoulders. The 'struck by lightning, sight restored' effect! But look here, he's recycled himself through that damn crystal fog of his instead."

"Which may well be an image of *this*." Norman Harper tapped the psychoscope, with its lab-grown crystals twinkling like great jewels. "Noel, I'm not in control of my own machine right now! It's interacting with him as though they're in symbiosis with each other. *It's* being operated by him, just as much as he's being operated on by it."

"You could always switch the power off."

"No," said Sally, from her seat at the readouts. "The shock, the trauma, could kill him. He's in a very strange state. It's as though he's hardly here at all. Except for the fantasies — which are vigorous enough. He's really possum."

" 'Possum' is a condition defined by Todhunter, not by us!"

"We may as well use the word. None of the other patients has reacted in quite this way."

"So far, we've only treated six people."

"And had six full cures," Norman Harper said defensively.

"I'm not criticising you, Norman. I'm not subtly attacking your psychoscope. Don't think that for one moment! Let's all *please* remember who we actually are. In my view there's a strong risk of transference in this case: we could start modelling our behaviour on our behaviour in the holos. Do you see the risk? *I* can feel the attraction. The infection. It's as though this masquerade reveals truths about ourselves, instead of being simply a fantasy."

"So that's what you feel, is it?"

"A barbed comment, Norman. Barbed."

Harper sighed. "Yes, you're right, damn it. Doubly right. I wouldn't have made a comment like that a few weeks ago."

"Equally fascinating is this wild death myth of his," began Resnick, hoping to regain firmer ground.

"Speaking of infections," interrupted Weinberger, "I guess he did have the grace to cure me."

'Whereas *I* murdered him?' Resnick rejected the thought hastily.

"In here, *he's* in charge of *you*, Nathan," he said calmly. "You aren't in charge of him. He can afford to be generous. But for my sins, *I'm* in charge of *him*. I'm evil. And somewhere inside of himself he knows that Norman is the actual one responsible for his predicament — technologically, I mean. Norman made the life-game possible — the rewriting of the world."

Harper raised an eyebrow at the mention of writing. He had a very low opinion of the poetry that Todhunter had foisted on to him.

"So he had *me* wipe Norman out?" Weinberger directed an apologetic glance towards Harper, who seemed to Resnick to flinch away. "And so I inherited the mantle of cage-maker, instead — in as much as the cage and everything it leads to is a reflection of this psychoscope of Norman's. Do you know, our big mistake was letting Todhunter even partly into our confidence before we put him under. Instead of just springing it upon him. And we did that because of his rational bouts. Because he'd helped in the House. Because, because."

"Yes, we did make it complicated for ourselves," agreed Resnick. He thought to himself, sternly, 'Nathan is *not* criticising or attacking me. He is *not*.'

"Getting involved in somebody else's psychosis has to be complicated."

"That's the point. We mustn't let ourselves get so caught up in it! This is a House of Life, not a House of Death. This isn't Egremont, it's Montegro."

"Ah yes, it's our very own House soap opera, isn't it?" said a voice. "When *will* he go to bed with one of the ladies?"

They had not heard Alice Huron push the glass door open. She stepped into the room now, clunking her chunky rings together by way of knocking.

Marta Bettijohn flushed, for she had taken her earphones off in time to hear. Alice regarded Marta with kindly amusement. Alice had accepted all of Todhunter's sexual innuendos about herself and Noel Resnick in good part, yet the man's stymied longings for Marta could only be an occasion for friendly hilarity. They all suspected that buxom, jolly Marta was still a virgin, and they had all privately (and perhaps not so privately) been wondering what the emotional impact would be on Marta when Todhunter finally bedded her, in technicolour holo. Which he had not done, however. So far, all that had come of it had been his dream fantasy of an inflatable Rubens nude of Marta; this had been embarrassing enough for her.

Standing tall, holding her chin high, Alice dominated the room.

"I asked you to meet me down here, Noel, because, well . . ."

"Because this is the centre of things?"

"Yes, isn't it just? I assumed Norman would be here."

"Oh, so you did know about the emergency?"

Alice laughed. "That's a line from the soap opera, Noel. It's an 'I know powerful secrets that you don't know' line." She frowned. "What emergency? What do you mean?"

Resnick indicated number two holo.

"It seems that I blew him up with a bundle of dynamite. But he didn't return from the fantasy. He's stuck." He explained what had happened.

"Oh dear. Oh dear, dear." She peered at the tiny dolls seated on the green baize lawn. "Well, I wanted this meeting —"

'Oh, so it's a meeting now? A meeting that *you* called?

'*Beware*!' Resnick reminded himself.

"— because I've been reviewing some of the implications of Norman's miraculous crystal transducers —"

Sarcasm? Norman Harper stiffened visibly, then relaxed, no doubt reminding himself, too, of the difference between the actual and the psychotic.

"— with the assistance of a very good physicist friend of mine up at the Neumann Centre."

Ah, so she had 'friends'? Was the man in question a very good friend — or just a very good physicist? Such delicate ambiguity!

168

Was the friend a man at all, or a woman? Resnick twitched his head, to try to shake some of the Todhunter mazes out of it.

"Item, the synaptic switching choices in Todhunter's head are being mirrored by the quantum electron shifts in these crystals which receive the brain signals and supply related output to the holo projectors via the computer."

Oh, she was at her most hoity-toity this afternoon!

'No, she isn't!'

"If the process wasn't conducted at the electron level," said Norman reasonably, "we'd have no way of processing the huge volume of information through into visible and audible play-outs."

"Yes indeed, and one little feature which my friend has pointed out about projecting a macrocosm — a world-reality, which is what this is — by using electron quantum jumps dictated by mental choices within our own world-reality, is that it is reliably theorised by the bright boys at Neumann and elsewhere that we're actually part of a multiple universe, a *multiverse* of infinitely many reality states — and, what's more, that every single quantum event evokes a whole separate coherent universe where that event never took place, as well as one where it did."

Her index finger forked left, right, left, tracing out branches of alternatives.

"So we *might* just have something more than a role-playing therapy machine here. In so far as every possible state of the universe is equally real, we might just have a simulator of this branching process on the large scale. A sampling device. A peephole, even."

"You surely aren't suggesting that Todhunter's world — this holo here — could be real? An alternative reality somewhere else?"

"One where all sorts of different choices have been made — because *mind* is the real determining factor in the branching process, according to the Neumann boys — so that Todhunter really is a guide in a House of Death!"

"Good heavens." Norman Harper stared at the audience seated on the lawn waiting, while Mayor Barnes held forth, for Norman Harper — poet — to rise and bid farewell. Exactly as in the first run of Father Todhunter's fantasy, before he had gained his wild

169

proof of the nature of death. Only, this time Father Todhunter — the unfrocked priest, former helper in the House of Life who had enticed children to his den and unfrocked them as their initiation into a secret society of minions, which would one day combat his imaginary enemies — only this time, he knew all about death . . . As well he should, having murdered one of his minions who was going to betray him. Which inevitably led to his own betrayal, and to the whole world turning against him. And the total snapping of his mind.

"Language doesn't describe this properly," explained Alice. "It isn't 'somewhere' else, you see. It's off at a million right angles to here, whilst still being 'here'. Only the maths can cope with transfinite dimensions. Through the psychoscope we might actually be in tune with one out of the myriad alternative states of existence — because 'somewhere' in transfinity *this too must exist*. Certainly it *could* exist."

"Be reasonable," said Weinberger. "That's a universe where little Deaths fly around rescuing the human race from a fate worse than death, on behalf of dead aliens. How on earth could that be a real universe?"

"There'll be much weirder universes than this one, Nathan. You can bet on it. But they'll be too different from ours for us even to conceive of them, let alone get in rapport with them — because they're based on choices that branched off aeons ago. This one's actually very close to ours — give or take the Death creatures, the crystal fog and so on."

"And little things such as the society of death, and the Sino-Soviet War," Weinberger reminded her.

"If it's a matter of choice," suggested Marta in hushed tones, "then a madman would choose a mad universe."

Alice smiled. "Maybe there are infinitely many mad universes. As well as infinitely many sane ones. Who's to say which infinity outnumbers the other?"

"I'll stick with the Montegro version of reality," said Marta stolidly. "Just so long as we don't let ourselves get confused by what happens in this, this —" •

"This life game," prompted Resnick.

"So long as, then we're all quite happy, thank you very much. Except for Father Todhunter." She sniffed. "Father to nobody, corrupter of many. It's odd that he didn't project his actual sexual misdemeanours into the . . . the universe he chose to echo."

"Oh but he did," said Weinberger. "He dumped them on my head, then he dismissed them as a slander. Actually, I'd be inclined to describe his sexual behaviour in this fantasy as fairly promising — in so far as sexual behaviour of any sort is considered promising in a priest! But that's *their* affair. No, he's attempting adult relationships. You'll note that he had to abolish the Church, to do so?"

"How can he possibly be engaged in behaviour that's promising, or unpromising, if he's simply echoing some alternative universe?" asked Marta, puzzled.

"This universe in the holo branches and rebranches all the time too," said Alice. "Todhunter made the big choice of which general reality best suited him, when he first entered it. Now that he's in there, he's faced with all the minor choices that he cares to make, every moment."

Norman Harper waved his hand.

"Watch the holo, will you? I'm due to speak. Noel's nearly finished, now."

"Shall we have audio?" asked Marta.

"Not likely! I can do without another performance of 'my' poetical works." Harper shook his head in mock exasperation. "The queer thing is, I actually did write poetry when I was a teenager, many moons ago. Oh, it was the usual adolescent stuff. Morbid stuff, mostly about death. Then I grew up."

"So you could indeed have lived like Goethe!" Resnick chuckled. "In another world! Wasn't Goethe a bit of a scientist, as well as a poet?"

"*That* was one of the most damned warped . . .! Do you know how the original of that Hölderlin poem goes? I looked it up. '*Lebt'ich, wie Götter* . . .' It means 'I have lived like the Gods.' Lived like Goethe, indeed!"

"But there aren't any Gods in Todhunter's universe," said Weinberger. "Just stick-insect angels and crystallized devils. Maybe . . . maybe a God only applies to some universes, and not to others?"

"There we are!" Harper pointed. "Up on my hind legs again, mouthing morbid banalities to the enthralled mob. Wait for it,

171

Nathan: your moment of glory soon."

Weinberger locked his hands together in his lap.

In silence they watched the homunculus of Norman Harper mouthing with his eyes shut.

The Weinberger homunculus scrambled to his feet and rushed towards the dais. He pointed a gun . . .

Norman Harper rocked in his seat, as though it was he who had been hit. He clasped his chest, agony and terror on his face.

"Oh *God*," he gasped.

He slid off the chair on to the floor.

Weinberger was kneeling by him in a moment, checking his pulse. Rolling Harper over, he began to thump his chest.

"It's a heart attack! Get the resuscitation unit here, Noel."

Resnick scrambled to the wall phone and dialled. He spoke briefly, then swiftly he opened the glass door and the outer door, pinning both back.

"He must have known about his heart!" cried Weinberger. "He must have had warnings! Why didn't he say?" He pressed his head to Harper's chest, devotedly. "Why did he stay to watch his own murder?"

"He had to stay," said Alice tightly, "to prove that he didn't believe in the evil eye — from some other reality!"

"I should have seen the signs," moaned Weinberger. "It's as though I killed him myself."

"You had nothing to do with this!" snapped Resnick. "*Nothing*, do you hear? Did you say 'killed'? Are you sure he's —?"

"Of course I'm sure."

"He isn't lost to us yet. Where's that unit!"

"For God's sake, what's *that*?" Marta pointed.

A red blur flickered up by the ceiling, high above the air-cushion bed where Todhunter lay entranced.

"What? There isn't anything . . . Oh my God," Resnick retreated.

Weinberger jumped aside as something almost-red and barely visible dived towards the body sprawled upon the floor. At the last moment it veered away, as though it had arrived too late.

There came a rush of footsteps and a bounce of rubber wheels in the corridor. As the two orderlies rushed in, propelling the resuscitation cart before them, the almost-red something fled out over their heads. Into the corridor, into the House, into Montegro and the world. The orderlies were too urgently occupied with hurrying the electric pads to Norman Harper's body to notice the creature — if indeed any outsider would have noticed it. They would have needed to know what to see.

While the orderlies were shocking Harper repeatedly to try to jolt his heart back to life, those who *had* seen Death stared at each other.

"It's got loose," said Resnick quietly, succumbing with a sinking feeling to the logic of Todhunter's world. "It has nowhere else to go in this dimension, does it, Alice? We'll have to build a cage to catch it."

"A cage for Death? But where do we get the pheromone? There's no such thing!"

"Maybe there is, if we look for it. Maybe there is now."

"I'm sorry, Mr Resnick," said one of the orderlies, standing up. "He's dead."

"Welcome to Egremont," said Marta raggedly. "Quite . . . quite an auspicious moment."

The orderly, Sorensen, stared at her as though she was mad.

In the holos, tiny marionette figures scrambled and panicked in the aftermath of the poet's murder.